# ACCUSED!

"Someone saw the whole thing. An old mountain man named Hyde."

"You have spoken to this Hyde personally?" I inquired.

"Sure have. He's right outside. You can ask him about it yourself." Without waiting for permission, Borke jumped up and was out the door. He returned with the scruffiest person I ever set eyes on.

"Jacob Hyde, at your service," the mountain man said courteously enough.

Colonel Templeton indicated another chair. "We would very much like to hear about the Shoshone attack on the trading post, Mr. Hyde."

"Glad to oblige. I recollect it like it was yesterday. But it ain't rightly fair to lay the blame on the Shoshones. It was a breed led 'em and he should be held to account as much as they should."

"The man who instigated the slaughter was part white? You're sure?"

"As sure as I'm breathin', Colonel," Hyde replied. "I saw him plain as day. The coon you want, the varmint who should be staked out and skinned alive for what he done, goes by the handle of Zachary King."

The *Wilderness* series:

# #41
# WILDERNESS
## BY DUTY BOUND

# David Thompson

LEISURE BOOKS  NEW YORK CITY

A LEISURE BOOK®

December 2003

Published by

Dorchester Publishing Co., Inc.
200 Madison Avenue
New York, NY 10016

ISBN 0-8439-5253-9

The name "Leisure Books" and the stylized "L" with design are
trademarks of Dorchester Publishing Co., Inc.

Printed in the United States of America.

Visit us on the web at www.dorchesterpub.com.

# #41
# WILDERNESS

## BY DUTY BOUND

# AUTHOR'S NOTE

*Most* WILDERNESS *books are based on the journals of Mountain Man Nate King and the diaries of his wife and daughter.*

*The story you are about to read is different in that its source is the private journal of Lieutenant Phillip J. Pickforth. The scion of a wealthy family, he left his life of luxury for the military, and after graduating from West Point, he was sent to Fort Leavenworth.*

*The Kings have a prominent part in his account. Few men had as pivotal an impact on their family, and to fully understand why, his side must be told.*

*Numerous references Pickforth made to his parents and siblings, and other personal matters, have been deleted. The rest of his narrative is largely intact, and the styling and wording are essentially his.*

*After careful consideration, I have retained his odd habit of talking to himself, or to an imaginary acquaintance, because of the insight it gives into his character.*

# Chapter One

I was adrift in the bliss of my afternoon nap when the orderly came to fetch me. It was Corporal Fiske, and I keenly resented his smirk.

"Sorry to disturb you, Lieutenant. But the colonel would take it as a personal favor if you could pry yourself from your pillow and pay him a visit."

Why do enlisted men feel compelled to belittle their superiors every chance they get? The corporal was typical. He looked down his nose at everyone above the rank of sergeant-major for no other reason than that they were officers and gentlemen. I gave him my sternest stare and indignantly responded, "I am certain those were not his exact words, Corporal. Repeat them verbatim."

"Ver-what sir?" He was genuinely puzzled.

"Verbatim means word for word, Corporal. Had

1

you stayed in school past the third grade, you would know that."

"Begging your pardon, sir, but I got as far as the sixth grade. My teacher, Miss Petry, could speak French and knew Latin, but she never used some of the words you throw at us. Sir."

He added that last as a slur against my four years at Princeton. I was aware some of the men were jealous of my higher learning, and although I tried not to make a show of my intellect, I couldn't help it they were such dunces. "The colonel's exact words, if you please."

" 'Have Lieutenant Pickforth report to me without delay,' " the corporal quoted.

By then I had my uniform buttoned and my hat on. "Let's not keep him waiting then, shall we?" I followed him across the parade ground to headquarters. Fiske announced my arrival and I was promptly admitted.

I must confess that Colonel Templeton was not an ideal officer. He was much too informal with the men, for one thing, and tended to be too lenient in dispensing discipline. Perhaps his age made him soft. In another year he was eligible to retire, and rumor had it that he planned to settle in Oregon Country and start a pear orchard. Now I ask you, is that any fit enterprise for a military man?

"Have a seat, Phillip," Templeton said with a negligent gesture at several chairs in front of his cluttered desk. That was another thing about him. He was much too sloppy in his habits.

"Thank you, sir," I said formally, and sat as stiff as a ramrod, as befit someone of rank.

Colonel Templeton rifled through a stack of papers, then looked up. He seemed deeply troubled and studied me a while before saying, "Do you like it here at Fort Leavenworth?"

"What is there to like, sir?" I answered honestly. "Our quarters are spartan, our food is barely worthy of the name. We waste far too much time in drills and on parade when we should be out in the field campaigning against hostiles. The heat is atrocious and saps a man's vitality, and the humidity is—" I had more to complain about, but he stopped me by lifting a hand.

"I take it that's 'no.'" The colonel sighed and leaned back. "I suppose to someone with your background conditions here would be primitive."

"Sir?"

"Come now, Phillip. We both know your family is enormously wealthy. Your father is a senator."

"My background, as you call it, sir, has no bearing on my assessment of the post. And for your edification, I have severed ties with my father and have not heard from him in several months."

"Oh?" Colonel Templeton tapped an envelope on his desk. "He writes me regularly to request updates on your performance."

I was so mad, I must have flushed red.

"Would you mind telling me why you severed ties?" When I did not answer right away, the colonel added, "Consider this a personal request, not an order. I never pry into the private affairs of those under me unless it directly relates to their duties."

"In that case, sir," I responded, "I would rather not say." I couldn't get over it. Once again my father was meddling, when I had made it as plain as plain can be that I wanted to make a go of it on my own.

"Very well," Colonel Templeton said. "Let's get on with it."

"With what, sir?" I said, eager to talk about something else.

"As you are probably aware, Captain Keane is on routine patrol. Captain Dugan is escorting a wagon train as far as South Pass, while Captain Tyler is dealing with some trouble involving the Pawnees. Captain Frazier is in the infirmary, and Captain Hindeman won't be back from his furlough for another ten days."

I did not quite see the point to all this, and made a comment to that effect.

"My point, Phillip, is that all of my experienced officers are otherwise engaged when I have need of them. Major Bannister is still here, of course, but when I leave for Washington in a week to testify at a government inquiry, he assumes command in my absence. So the assignment I have in mind must be given to a junior officer. Are you interested?"

I almost came out of my chair. "Need you ask, sir?" I had been there four months and had not once been sent beyond the gate.

"To be honest, Phillip, I haven't quite made up my mind. It's extremely dangerous, if I say so myself. It would entail leading a column to the Rocky Mountains and conducting an investigation into an alleged massacre."

The Rockies! I could have whooped with glee. Long ago I had heard wondrous and exciting tales about those faraway ramparts and the legion of fierce beasts and bloodthirsty heathens inhabiting them. I would give anything to see the Rockies with my own eyes. To venture where few whites had ever gone. But to avoid appearing childish, I restrained my enthusiasm and said, "A massacre, sir?"

"Yes. Word has reached us that a trading post was overrun and the civilians slaughtered."

"How many were killed, sir?"

"Seven, according to our informant."

"And the culprits, sir?"

"Supposedly the Shoshones." Colonel Templeton paused. "Are you at all familiar with the various tribes, Phillip?"

"I've read all the required reports, sir." I racked my brain for every mention I ever heard of them, and one kernel of information stood out. "Aren't the Shoshones supposed to be friendly, sir?"

"None friendlier. They've gone out of their way to maintain peaceful relations with us. There has never been a single instance of a Shoshone attacking a white man. Which, as you can readily understand, makes our informant's information suspect."

"Who is this informant and when do I meet him, sir?"

"His name is Borke. Phineas Borke. His brother was head of the trading post. He's due back here in two hours. I expect you to be here to hear what he has to say."

"With pleasure, sir."

The colonel seemed to choose his next words with care. "We must proceed with caution in a circumstance like this, Phillip. It would not do to incite a friendly tribe to violence if they have been unjustly accused." Rising, he turned to a large wall map. "Look at it, Phillip. Thousands of square miles of untamed wilderness, over which we're expected to preserve order with a few hundred men. It's an impossible task. The army is talking about building more forts farther west, an action I've endorsed for years, but until then Fort Leavenworth is the last bastion between the Mississippi River and California. We have been entrusted with a powder keg that might blow up in our faces at any moment."

I was well aware of the situation and mildly resented being lectured to, but he was my commanding officer and I was obligated to endure it.

The colonel reached up to tap a spot high on the map. "Up here we have the Blackfeet, or, to be more exact, the Blackfoot Confederacy." He tapped another spot. "Here we have the Sioux. Here the Cheyenne. Here the Arapahos. Here are the Utes. Down here the Apaches. In Texas, the Comanches. Tribes who have shown themselves to be inimical to white intrusion."

I had to admit that the colonel's vocabulary at times was equal to mine, which is no mean feat of mental accomplishment.

"Mark my words, Phillip. As time marches on and more and more of our people seek their fortunes in the West, more and more of them will lose their lives to unfriendly Indians. It's inevitable. Just as it's inevitable we can't keep a lid on things at our current state of readiness. There should be twenty forts stretched from Canada to Mexico, and even that would not begin to give settlers the protection they need."

All this was old hat. I had listened to his pet spiel many an evening at the mess hall.

"Discretion is called for, Phillip. We must try, as much as possible, to remain on friendly relations with the Indians. Some, like the Blackfeet, hate us outright and will never live in peace. Others, like the Shoshones, have offered us the hand of friendship, and we are duty-bound to reach out and accept that hand."

I cleared my throat. "I understand what you're saying, sir. I mustn't permit myself to jump to conclusions."

Colonel Templeton looked at me. "There is more to being an officer than following orders. Good officers learn to think for themselves. To go by the book, but to bend the book when the situation warrants."

"Bend the rules, sir?" I was aghast. The very idea went against everything I had been taught, and, indeed, against my own temperament. Rules were made to be obeyed. Without exception. Without question.

"That will be all for now, Phillip," the colonel dismissed me. "Report back in two hours and I will introduce you to Mr. Borke."

Far be it from me to be critical of others, but Phineas Borke was as slovenly an individual as I ever met. He was round of body and round of face and had a greasy, sweaty complexion that was most unappealing. I didn't let on how I felt when we were introduced, and after shaking his hand, took the proffered seat.

Borke wore homespun clothes in need of several washings to be anywhere near clean. His fingernails were filthy, his boots scuffed. When he talked, I noticed he had a piece of food stuck between his front teeth. At one point he casually flicked it out, and it landed close enough to my chair to make me queasy.

"As I was just tellin' your superior, here, Lieutenant, I've come to the army as a last resort. My brother's blood screams for vengeance, and you're the only jaspers in a position to see he gets it."

"You were close to your brother, I take it?" I asked.

"Like two peas in a pod," Borke declared. "Why, if it hadn't been for a busted leg, I'd have gone with him. And right now I'd be pushin' up grass, same as him. God rest his soul."

"Perhaps you would be so kind as to repeat your story to the lieutenant?" Colonel Templeton suggested.

"Glad to." Borke hooked his pudgy thumbs around his suspenders. "You see, my older brother Artemis had himself a brainstorm a while back. He'd heard about how much money tradin' posts make and figured he could turn a hefty profit if he could set one up where it would be safe from rovin' hostiles. Well, word has it there aren't any Injuns anywhere friendlier than the Shoshones, so he reckoned to set his tradin' post up in their territory."

"His proposal sounds eminently feasible to me," I commented.

Borke cocked his head. "What did you just say?"

"I said it sounds like a good idea.

"Oh. You could have fooled me." Borke cleared his throat. "Anyhow, brother Artemis rounded up some good boys to go with him. Six mother's sons as fearless as he was. They took ten pack animals loaded with trade goods and whatnot, and struck off for the Green River country."

"Without letting us know," Colonel Templeton commented.

"The last time I saw him," Borke went on, "Artemis shook my hand and promised to come back with more money than either of us had ever seen in all our born days." He stopped and bowed his head. "I miss him somethin' terrible."

I could see the man was grief-stricken, but Colonel Templeton said rather harshly, "How did your brother plan to acquire all this money? The fur trade collapsed years ago. And not much else the Indians can trade is of much value."

"It's no secret, though, that tradin' posts generally make sizable profits," Borke stated.

"They should," Colonel Templeton said. "Most traders mark up their merchandise anywhere from twenty-five to fifty percent, the dishonest ones even more."

"Wait a second, Colonel. Are you implyin' Artemis was up to no good? That he was fixin' to cheat the Injuns?"

"Don't put words in my mouth, Mr. Borke. I simply noted your brother's expectations were unrealistic. Be that as it may, we view your alleged account of a massacre with the utmost concern." The colonel was now studying Borke as intently as he previously studied me. "Which brings to mind a pertinent question. How is it you learned the details of the atrocity when your brother and all those with him were slain?"

"Someone saw the whole thing. An old mountain man named Hyde. He heard about the tradin' post and rode down from his cabin in the high country to pay it a visit. He got there just as the shootin' commenced."

"You have spoken to this Hyde personally?" I inquired.

"Sure have. He's right outside. You can ask him about it yourself." Without waiting for permission, Borke jumped up and was out the door. He returned with the scruffiest person I ever set eyes on, a scarecrow in worn buckskins with a scraggly gray beard that fell to his thin waist.

"Jacob Hyde, at your service," the mountain man said courteously enough.

Colonel Templeton indicated another chair. "We would very much like to hear about the Shoshone attack on the trading post, Mr. Hyde."

"Glad to oblige. I recollect it like it was yesterday. But it ain't rightly fair to lay the blame on the Shoshones. It was a breed led 'em, and he should be held to account as much as they should."

"The man who instigated the slaughter was part white? You're sure?"

"As sure as I'm breathin', Colonel," Hyde replied. "I saw him plain as day. The coon you want, the varmint who should be staked out and skinned alive for what he done, goes by the handle of Zachary King."

# Chapter Two

We departed Fort Leavenworth three days later. Twenty-four soldiers had been placed under my command. The colonel wanted to give me an entire company; he told me so himself. But there weren't enough men to spare, so I ended up with barely half a platoon.

A few words about those under me.

Sergeant Wheatridge was the ranking noncommissioned officer. A career man, he had been on more Indian campaigns than all the privates put together. He sported bushy sideburns and a great mustache, was a foot taller than I and quite broad of shoulder and chest, and was, I must admit, the toughest individual it has ever been my experience to meet. The man was made of iron. On marches he could go all day and all night and not tire, and on horseback he could ride forever. He was an excellent marksman. When he gave an order, the men snapped to. In short, Wheatridge was the most indispensable member of my command, next to myself. Small wonder Colonel Templeton mentioned him when he took me aside shortly before we rode out.

"I've given you the best sergeant I have, Phillip. Listen to him. His advice is invaluable. When in doubt, rely on his judgment."

Yes, the colonel was wise in assigning Sergeant Wheatridge, but his choice of a corporal left considerable to be desired. Much to my chagrin, it turned out to be Corporal Fiske. Granted, he, too, had seen his share of Indian campaigns, but the man had demonstrated a strong dislike toward me personally, and I thought it was asking for aggravation to take him along. I mentioned this to Templeton, who gave me a most peculiar look.

"You'll take Fiske because Wheatridge requested him, and that's that."

Of the privates, all but three were under twenty years of age. Smooth-faced boys, none of whom enlisted because it was their patriotic duty. Some signed up out of a sense of grand adventure. Others because they were dirt poor and the fourteen dollars a month the army paid seemed to them a fair exchange for the possible loss of their lives.

Ordinarily a scout would be assigned. But in this instance Colonel Templeton saw fit to allow Jacob Hyde to guide us, at twenty-five dollars a month. Phineas Borke also came along, and insisted on bringing two friends.

We expected to be gone for months. Consequently, I was allotted eight pack animals. The colonel instructed me to live off the land as much as practical, and except for essentials like coffee and tea, to resort to my supplies only when I had no other recourse.

Our uniforms were the latest issue. A few years previous, the Army had stopped the use of flintlock rifles and converted to percussion. We were outfitted with the U.S. Rifleman's outfit, model 1841. Our single-shot rifles were accurate out to two hundred yards in the hands of a skilled shooter, of which, admittedly, there were all too few.

This, then, paints an accurate portrait of my command on that fateful June morning as I rode past the review stand on my way to the gate. I gave my snappiest salute to Colonel Templeton, and within moments we were under way.

It was common practice to go a short distance the first day. This was done so when camp was made, if anything had been forgotten, it could easily be retrieved before pushing on into the vast unknown. I went ten miles and gave the order to stop. We spent a peaceful evening. Sergeant Wheatridge reported that all was in order, and the next morning we were under way in earnest.

As yet I had not had much opportunity to question Phineas Borke or my new scout, a lapse I intended to remedy at the earliest opportunity. The second evening, I invited them to my tent, along with the good sergeant, and after a passable meal of roast venison and a glass of wine from my personal stock, I turned inquisitor.

"So tell me, Mr. Borke. Do you or Mr. Hyde have any idea why your brother and his men were wiped out?"

"Since when do Injuns need an excuse to kill whites?" Borke responded.

I was already annoyed with him. During our meal he displayed the most atrocious table manners. He ate with his mouth open, chomping like a bear, and nearly spoiled my appetite. To have him be so flippant only annoyed me more. "That might be true of the Apaches or the Comanches. But the Shoshones have never killed white men before."

"Injuns ain't no different than anyone else," Borke said defensively. "The Shoshones saw a chance to get their miserable red hands on my brother's trade goods, and took it."

Sergeant Wheatridge had barely uttered four words the whole meal, but now he fixed those piercing blue eyes of his on Borke. "Begging your pardon, but I've met a few Shoshones. And never once did they show ill will to us whites."

Borke opened his mouth to say something, but Jacob Hyde beat him to it. "I agree, Sergeant. In all my decades in the mountains, I've never had any trouble with the Shoshones. Maybe the blame should be placed on Zach King." He lowered his voice and grinned. "You know what they say about breeds."

Since no one elaborated, I asked, "What do they say, Mr. Hyde?"

"Mixed blood is tainted blood. Ask anyone out here, they'll tell you that breedin' white and red brings out the worst of both."

I had attended Princeton. I knew a little about the natural sciences. So I told him straight out, "That's preposterous, sir. It's tantamount to superstition."

"Call it what you want, Lieutenant. But there ain't anyone on the frontier worth his salt who trusts a breed any further than he can chuck a grown buff. And this Zach King is one of the worst. A white-hater from the day his squaw of a mother vomited him out her womb."

"He's also the son of Nate King, as I recollect," Sergeant Wheatridge remarked.

It had a strange effect. Borke and Hyde glanced at each other, and neither seemed to know quite what to say until Borke blurted, "Heard of him, have you?"

"Who hasn't?" was the sergeant's rejoinder.

I trusted that I could be forgiven my ignorance since I was, after all, relatively new to this. "I haven't. Who is he, Sergeant?"

"A mountain man, sir. One of the first. Got his start as a free trapper, and when the beaver trade died, he took to guiding wagon trains and the like. They say there isn't a more honorable man anywhere."

Jacob Hyde tugged at his beard. "That doesn't necessarily mean the son is cut from the same cloth. Many a rotten apple has dropped from a healthy tree."

"All this is speculation, at best," I inserted. "We have hundreds of miles to travel before we can begin our investigation, so we might as well let the matter drop until we reach the Rockies."

Borke grinned that oily grin of his. "Fine by me, Lieutenant. As I've said all along, all I'm interested in is seein' justice done. My dear, departed brother would do the same for me."

He and Hyde and their two associates soon excused themselves, and I was left alone with Sergeant Wheatridge. The sergeant had dallied over his wine, odd for a drinking man. As soon as they were gone, he leaned toward me and said so only I heard, "I don't trust them, sir."

"How's that, Sergeant?"

"Borke and Hyde, sir. Their tale is mighty suspicious. No son of Nate King would do what they claim."

"Know this for a fact, do you?" I asked, more than a little facetiously.

Wheatridge sat back and was quiet a minute. "Eighteen years ago there was a raw recruit who didn't know one end of a bayonet from the other. One day on summer campaign this boy was ordered to hunt for fresh meat. He shot a doe, but he made the mis-

14

take of straying too far off and couldn't make it back to camp by nightfall. He wasn't worried, because he knew his captain wouldn't desert him. Since he was hungry, and not knowing any better, he made a big fire and rigged a spit and ate until he was fit to burst." He sipped some wine. "What he didn't know was that four Bloods had spotted the fire. They waited until he was good and drowsy from gorging himself, then they jumped him."

"My word."

"He was scared, sir. So scared it was a wonder he didn't wet himself. The Bloods stripped him naked and staked him out right there. But they didn't kill him right off. They weren't in any hurry." Wheatridge chuckled. "No, what they did was sit down and help themselves to his doe."

I could well imagine how the young trooper must have felt. Alone, defenseless, and at the mercy of hostiles—it was every soldier's worst nightmare.

Wheatridge resumed his tale. "Toward midnight they took burning brands from the fire and amused themselves by jabbing the red-hot ends against the boy's arms and legs. He did his best not to cry out, but once or twice he couldn't help himself. When they tired of their play, he feared he was in for worse, but they did the last thing he expected. They went to sleep. Needless to say, he spent the rest of the night in dread."

I was completely absorbed, reliving it as if I were there.

"Came the dawn, and the Bloods argued with one another. Two wanted to kill him outright. One even went so far as to draw a knife and press the blade to his throat. But the other two wanted to take him back to their village. So they bound his wrists behind his back, threw a rope over his neck, and led him off like a dog on a leash."

Every soldier feared the prospect of being taken alive. Any who claimed differently were liars or braggarts.

"The young soldier had to walk fast to keep up with their horses, and it wasn't long before the skin on his feet was peeled away and his feet were so cut and bloody, they were bright red. At midday the Bloods stopped at a stream. He collapsed from exhaustion, and the next thing he knew, something spooked their horses and the Bloods ran off after them. The Bloods didn't bother taking him. They knew he wasn't going anywhere." Sergeant Wheatridge finished his wine.

"And?" I coaxed when he didn't continue quickly enough. "Speak up, man. What fate befell him?"

"He was lying there in the grass, too exhausted to move, when someone grabbed him from behind and slung him onto a horse, belly down. He never heard a sound, and it happened so fast, he figured it was a Blood. Then a white man whispered in his ear, 'I'll get you out of this alive. Don't you worry.' And that white man was as good as his word. They gave those Bloods the slip as slick as you please, and his rescuer put some kind of ointment on the soldier's feet to help them heal, and even gave the soldier his spare set of buckskins."

I had not attended Princeton for nothing. "That young soldier was you?"

"That it was, sir. And the man who saved me, the trapper who put his own life at risk to save mine, was Nate King. Whose wife, by the way, is Shoshone." Sergeant Wheatridge rose. "Something to think about, eh?"

"Indeed," I agreed, returning his salute.

Over the next several weeks, as I became more acquainted with Phineas Borke and his companions, the less highly I thought of them. Jacob Hyde I have already described. He was friendly enough, and always willing to share his extensive knowledge of the wilds, but there was something about him, a shiftiness, if you will, that made me think of a wary rodent.

The other two were named Clemens and Sewell. Stamped from the same crude mold, they were uncouth characters, as slovenly in their habits and appearance as Borke. Neither ever had much to say in my presence. The best I could gather was that they were vagabonds who had spent a good deal of time in the bayou country down around New Orleans until recently, when they hooked up with Borke.

My men were in good spirits. And why shouldn't they be, when game was abundant and we never lacked for water? To give credit where credit is due, Jacob Hyde not only had the location of every creek and spring memorized, but he also possessed an uncanny knack for finding food for the supper table.

For my own part, I must admit to equal measures of keen anticipation and deep disappointment. I was one of those who enlisted for the adventure, and as one uneventful day after another went by, I found myself hoping something would happen. I know, I know. We must always be careful what we ask for.

Finally a noteworthy event occurred, but not the kind you might think.

One afternoon Jacob Hyde came hurrying back from point to inform me we were nearing an Indian village. I immediately turned to Sergeant Wheatridge and ordered him to have the men check their rifles and pistols.

# David Thompson

"They're Kanzas Indians, Lieutenant," Jacob Hyde said in a tone that implied it explained everything.

"So?"

Sergeant Wheatridge understood, even if I didn't. "Our rifles won't be needed, sir. You'll see why soon enough."

That was the day I discovered there is no limit to the depths to which humankind can sink.

Here I was, accustomed to sleeping on soft silk sheets and to always wearing the finest of clothes. For most of my life I had lived in a fabulous mansion on a lush estate that rivaled the Garden of Eden. And now I was to come face-to-face with the poorest of the poor, with Man as he must have been after the Fall. For surely there are no more pitiable human beings anywhere than the Kanzas, or Caw, Indians.

I was aghast. The pathetic wretches lived in small hovels. Huts, I guess you would call them, made of branches and straw and dirt, a few covered partly by hides, but in the main they weren't fit habitation for swine, let alone entire families.

These Kanzas styled themselves farmers and had learned to cultivate beans, corn, and pumpkins, among other vegetables, but they barely grew enough to fill their bellies.

The village we had stumbled on contained some sixty to seventy men, women, and children, all of whom gathered to gawk at us. I had often read about the steel-thewed warriors of the plains, but these were not them. The men were scrawny to the point of being malnourished, the women little better. Yet they stood straight and proud, and their leader, or chief, greeted us warmly and invited us to stay the night so they could hold a special celebration in our honor.

18

Through my interpreter, Mr. Hyde, I politely declined.

"Unbelievable," I commented to Sergeant Wheatridge as we rode off. "It's a wonder none of the more savage tribes haven't wiped them out."

"The Kanzas are looked down on as too weak to bother with, sir. But with us it will be different, and in another week we'll be in hostile country."

Lord help me, I couldn't wait.

# Chapter Three

The next tribe we encountered, though, were not much of an improvement on the Kanzas. They were called the Otoes. Their huts were somewhat sturdier. At least I had the impression they wouldn't blow away in a strong wind. And the Otoes wore slightly more clothes. But overall they were about as savage as rabbits.

Sergeant Wheatridge suggested we trade for some of the crops these wretches grew, and remembering the colonel's advice, I gladly took his. We procured several bushels of early corn, beans, and a large quantity of turnips, which I detest but which Sergeant Wheatridge assured me we would sorely need before too many more miles. For although we didn't lack for water, since we were following the Republican River, game became surprisingly scarce. Jacob Hyde told me this was normal, that from here on until we reached the Rockies, finding enough to eat would be a challenge. He didn't exaggerate.

19

## David Thompson

Although I sent out hunting parties daily, most evenings they came back empty-handed, or with a coyote or a hawk to show for their effort. Hardly appetizing fare. Jacob Hyde and Sergeant Wheatridge shot an antelope on separate occasions, and it disturbed me to see how my half-starved men tore into the meat when it was barely cooked, and how, like ravenous wolves, they gnawed each morsel down to bone.

One evening, after five days with no more to live on than a few small fish and quail, Corporal Fiske came to where Sergeant Wheatridge and I were huddled over one of my maps.

"Sorry to disturb you, sir. But could I have a word with the sergeant in private, if you please?"

I turned to him. Fiske was always polite, but the scorn lurking in his eyes betrayed his true feelings. "Whatever you have to say to the good sergeant you may also say in my presence, Corporal."

He hesitated and glanced at Wheatridge, whose chin bobbed. "Very well, sir. I thought it best to report that a few of the men have been grumbling about deserting. Nothing serious, mind you, sir. As yet, anyway."

Nothing serious, indeed! Desertion was a chronic problem, and not one the army smiled on. Granted, the conditions under which the enlisted men toiled were at times trying. It could not have been appealing, for instance, to shovel horse manure. But they took an oath and they were obligated by duty and honor to fulfill it.

The army liked to keep the exact number of desertions hushed up, but Colonel Templeton had confided in me that in an average year, Fort Leavenworth suffered at least fifteen. Keep in mind that when an enlisted man departed for easier pastures, his uniform, equipment and horse often went with him, at a cost to the military of up to three hundred dollars per desertion. Multiply that by the total and you can see how costly the practice was.

I resolved on the spot to crush this incipient rebellion before it spread any further. "Have the men assembled," I commanded Corporal Fiske. "I will speak to them."

Sergeant Wheatridge cleared his throat. "That might not be necessary, sir. I can take the blowhards aside one by one and convince them of the error of their ways."

I drew myself up to my full height. "I am the officer in charge. I will handle this breach as I see fit." At Fiske I barked, "Assemble them, and be quick about it."

The recruits were a sullen lot, and I did not bandy words. "It has come to my attention that some of you entertain the notion of deserting. Be assured that any such attempt will be dealt with in a summary and harsh manner." I gave them a few seconds to let that sink in. "Under army regulations, I am authorized to deal with deserters as I see fit. I will have you tracked down, bound hand and foot, and brought back. You will then be given thirty lashes, stripped of all privileges, and your pay suspended. Upon our return to Fort Leavenworth, you will be brought up on formal charges, and I can promise you, as surely as I am standing here, that you will spend from five to ten years in a military prison." I paused again, then raked them with what I intended to be a withering look of reproach. "So then, who wants to desert first?"

They had never before seen me angry, truly angry, and my denunciation left them speechless.

"Very well, then," I said when no one spoke. "Let's not hear any more such nonsense. You are all grown men and you have a duty to perform, and by God, I expect you to damn well perform it. That uniform you wear is not for show. It stands as a symbol of the great nation in whose cause you have enlisted, and you owe it to yourself to be as true to your country as you can."

In the silence that ensued, Sergeant Wheatridge's deep voice crisply declared, "That will be all, gentlemen. You are dismissed."

Whether my talk had any lasting effect or not, I cannot say. But I can record that our expedition did not suffer one desertion. They stuck with me to the end, and given what lay in store, that alone was remarkable.

At Jacob Hyde's urging, we left the vicinity of the Republican River and trekked northwest toward the Platte. It was the low point of our plains crossing. The men were gaunt and weary, and some had taken to licking their lips when they looked at their own horses. Campaigners were sometimes compelled to eat their animals in order to survive, but I refused to give my consent. We were cavalry, not foot soldiers.

Then came the morning we struck the Platte River, and almost immediately Jacob Hyde and Sergeant Wheatridge spotted a herd of deer in the timber. That evening we dined on four does and an antlerless buck, and never was there a finer feast fit for king or pauper. I let the men gorge themselves. Some overdid it to such an extent, they became sick.

Not a week later we stumbled on five elk and brought down two of them. I had most of the meat dried and salted for future use, and thus replenished, we continued deeper into the untamed heart of the primitive.

As yet, I had not set eyes on a hostile, nor had I seen any buffalo. I mentioned the latter one afternoon as we were winding along the sluggish Platte, and Jacob Hyde happened to be with us.

"Most buffs are well south of here this time of year, Lieutenant. The big brutes migrate, just like ducks and geese. We still might see some, though, if we're lucky."

I hoped we were. By my calculations we had traveled over nine hundred miles, with another four to five hundred to go, and it would be a travesty of the natural order if we should go the whole distance without once spotting the animal most associated with the prairie. Apparently the Almighty agreed, because the very next morning Hyde came galloping back to report that a small herd of buffalo was directly ahead. Leaving the men with Corporal Fiske, I rode on with Sergeant Wheatridge, the scout, and Phineas and his companions, to a low knoll. And there below us, at long last, were my buffalo.

Hyde's idea of a small herd was not the same as mine. Where I expected a few hundred, at most, my wondering eyes beheld many thousands, their dark forms dotting the plain for as far as I could see. Some were grazing. Others lay chewing their cuds, if indeed buffalo resemble cows in that respect. Still others were rolling around in what Hyde informed me were "wallows." They presented quite an idyllic scene, as picturesque as any painting but all the more real for the sound of their snorts and grunts and their pawing of the ground, and, too, for their smell.

I have long had an aversion to foul odors. My father called me a fanatic in this regard, but then, his opinion of me in general left considerable to be desired. I freely admit I do not like the stink of sweaty feet and armpits, nor the reek of manure or the ends out of which the manure comes. But show me a sane person who does! So as we sat there on that knoll, with the breeze blowing from the buffalo to us, I crinkled my nose in disgust.

"Not Nature's bouquet, are they, Lieutenant?" Jacob Hyde said. "The only thing worse is a grizzly's den after a griz has been cooped up all winter. One whiff and you can hardly breathe."

"Been in many grizzly dens, have you?"

"A few. I've killed a few griz in my time, too. Not as many as Nate King, but no one will ever match his tally. That's why the Injuns call him Grizzly Killer."

Hyde said the last with blatant bitterness, which piqued my curiosity. "It sounds to me as if you are not all that fond of him."

"I'm not," Hyde said before he could catch himself.

"Might I inquire why?"

"It's personal." Jerking on his reins, he rode back toward the column with Borke and the other two.

Sergeant Wheatridge's brow was furrowed in thought. "Interesting, sir, wouldn't you say?"

"I would indeed. Perhaps there is more to his allegation against the Kings than he has let us believe." But how to learn the truth? I wondered. That was the dilemma confronting me.

We headed back. Hyde was huddled with Borke, Clemens, and Sewell. They stopped talking the moment I rode up. "What do you recommend, scout? Do we sit here and wait for the herd to move on, or do we go around them?"

"It could be days before they move on," Hyde said. "Going around will only take us a few hours out of our way, so maybe that's best."

I cared for neither option. Both meant delays, and at this point reaching the site of the alleged massacre was foremost on my mind. "What if we were to go through them?" I proposed. It seemed sensible enough. The buffalo did not seem the least belligerent when we were watching them, except for a few bulls that snorted at one another while gouging the ground with their great hooves.

"We could go through, yes," Hyde said, "but it's mighty dangerous. One cough or sneeze can send the whole bunch to stampedin'."

"He's right, sir," Corporal Fiske made bold to say. "And if you've ever seen those beasts with their dander up, as I have, you'd know there aren't enough big words to describe it."

I construed his comment as yet another slur against my degree, and as I have often done when someone pushes me too far, I pushed back. "We're going through. Inform the men." I looked to Sergeant Wheatridge to see if he objected. He didn't appear pleased at my decision, but he didn't voice opposition to it, either, which I took as a sign my idea held a pound of merit.

That amount, however, had dwindled to an ounce by the time we crossed the rise. Once again I beheld the great shaggy brutes in all their formidable splendor. My eyes were drawn to their wicked horns and to their more than imposing size. They were huge, these bovines of the plains. Perfectly capable of bowling over a cavalry mount and disemboweling it with the same ease you or I might gut a trout.

"To do this right, we'd better string out in single file," Jacob Hyde suggested. "I'll lead. Let your boys know there can't be any talkin' or whistlin' or singin'.

And warn 'em the horses might get skittish so keep a tight rein."

I commanded Sergeant Wheatridge to spread word down the line. When we were ready, I signaled, and we rode straight toward the herd. Hyde was in front of me, Phineas Borke and his two shadows behind. It was not until we were a rifle's shot away that doubt assailed me.

If you have never been close to buffalo, truly close, so close you can see their nostrils flare and their dark eyes swivel in their sockets when they look at you, you can't possibly appreciate how fearsome they are. Large males are over six feet high at the shoulder. Add to that their distinctive humps and their ugly horns and their peculiar tails with tufts at the end, and they are without question creatures the Almighty created in one of His more somber moods.

I have heard buffalo compared to cattle, but the comparison falls short. Cows are docile creatures; buffalo have explosive temperaments and are capable of the most astonishing violence. As the enlisted men like to say, they are half a ton of pure nasty. And here I was, leading my men into a herd of these monsters!

It was too late to reverse my decision, which was just as well since it's viewed as a sign of weakness in a superior. I forced myself to sit tall in the saddle and regarded the bison with what I hoped was a totally fearless air. Jacob Hyde was also a monument to calm, but when I glanced over my shoulder, I saw that Borke and his friends were as nervous as cats in a dog kennel. They constantly glanced from side to side while nervously fingering their rifles. I prayed they wouldn't do anything foolish; one shot would place us all in peril.

A stampede; the word reverberated in my head like echoing thunder. There were so many buffalo, we would be trampled under their flailing hooves like so much wheat under a thresher, reducing us to pulped chaff. We could not possibly withstand them. Or outrun them. Or elude them.

It was only then that the full magnitude of my mistake in judgment hit me. I had, in effect, potentially doomed every member of my undersized platoon, and all because I let anger dictate a decision. Of the many follies officers can commit, this was arguably the worst. When lives are at stake, it ill befits a leader to behave in petty fashion. At West Point we were taught to keep our emotions in check, to always keep a clear head and rely on logic. By acting rashly, I had gone against a cardinal precept, and it was my men who might pay for my lapse.

I am not ashamed to admit I was sweating as I never sweated before. It poured off me in great drops, soaking my uniform and causing my back to itch. I wanted to scratch. I wanted to mop my forehead. But I was afraid to move my arms for fear of inciting the unthinkable.

Many buffalo stopped what they were doing to stare. Some snorted and stomped, and a few bulls lowered their heads and shook their great horns. One trotted toward me but stopped twenty feet off and rumbled deep in its massive chest. I swear, the short hairs at the nape of my neck prickled.

I did not realize my mouth had gone dry until I tried to swallow. Nor that I had held my breath until I let it out.

You will think me childish, but as frightening as the buffalo were, these were grand moments. I was filled with a heady mix of fright and excitement that was intoxicating. Maybe it was the prospect of imminent death. Maybe it was merely being so close to these shaggy behemoths. But I felt more alive than I ever did.

On we rode, Jacob Hyde threading us through gaps in the herd like a master seamstress threading a needle. How long it took us, I cannot rightly judge. But eventually came the moment when the last of the buffalo were behind us and we reined up to gaze back and marvel at our deliverance.

In my exuberant mood, I grinned at my men and declared, "There now. That wasn't so bad, was it?"

For some odd reason, not one of them smiled at my little joke.

# Chapter Four

What does it say about the human race that we can live in the same house with someone day after day, week after week, and not get to know them any better than we do a tree in our front yard?

Did I say house? I meant company, because although by this time I had spent weeks with Phineas Borke and his friends, I knew them no better than I did the moment I initially set eyes on them. They were much too secretive for my liking. On various occasions I tried to draw them into conversation about their past, and specifically about Borke's dealings with his brother, but he always proved evasive or changed the subject.

Jacob Hyde was no better. He would talk freely about wildlife and the wilderness but would not offer so much as a tidbit about his personal life or give me an inkling of why he was so bitter toward Nate King.

Nor, I am ashamed to admit, did I get to know my own men all that well. I tried. I truly tried. In the evenings I would on occasion mingle with them to sound out their feelings and thoughts, but they inevitably became as tight-lipped as clams. I think my being an officer was to blame. Enlisted men are notoriously uncomfortable around their superiors. Why that should be is a mystery. Perhaps it is the ages-old aversion to authority. Lord knows, I have been guilty of that in my own life, but not without more than adequate cause.

I mention all this to show that the state of affairs was little different near the end of our crossing of the prairie than it had been when we started out.

We were paralleling the course of the Platte River, and although obtaining food was still a daily challenge, as we neared the vicinity of the foothills game once again became abundant and our meals more regular.

On a warm morning early in September, shortly after we broke camp and headed out, Jacob Hyde trotted back to tell me he had smelled the smoke from a cookfire ahead, and that we should proceed with caution since we were in the heart of hostile territory. Accordingly, I ordered the men to be vigilant and keep their rifles across their pommels, and we cautiously advanced another half a mile.

I must say, at this point, that I could understand why some men became so enamored of the West. I found the countryside picturesque in the extreme. Imagine, if you will, pockets of prairie so covered with wild flowers of every shade and color as to present the image of a vibrant rainbow. Or imagine woods so green and lush and dense that the merest whisper is like a thunderclap in their stillness. Or, again, high cliffs and bluffs of rock and clay that rear from the plain like fingers jutting accusingly at God, and which, in the bright reflected light of the blazing sun, become beacons, lighthouses in a sea of grass.

My words do not convey the marvelous beauty, the monumental wonder. For that I apologize. I am not as adept with words as my cousin, the poet, who can weave the most beautiful poetical tapestries from the most mundane of events. The best I can do is relate what I saw as I saw it, and hope that in some small measure I convey the true grandeur, or horror, of what I encountered.

Anyway, on this particular morning, we advanced until I, too, smelled the acrid scent of wood smoke, although we did not see any, and presently, through the trees, we beheld a small fire and a man squatted on his haunches beside it, watching us approach. And what a man! If I live to be a hundred I will never meet another individual so gaudily attired. You will think I am exaggerating when I describe him, but I am not. But here. I will let you judge for yourself, and describe him as best my paltry powers enable me.

He had stringy white hair, this apparition, with a face with more wrinkles than an old prune or fig. His ragged beard was in a tangle. His right eye was brown, but where his left should be was a thick ridge of scar tissue. All this alone was remarkable, but I have not yet really begun to present his true image.

He wore a broad-sleeved purple shirt the likes of which had not been in style in more years than I can remember. His pants were buckskin. His boots were the high-heeled, knee-high, square-toed type once fashionable in France. Over his shirt he wore a red velvet coat with brass buttons. I kid you not. Yet that was not all. His hat was of the wide-brimmed Spanish style, with a high crown. And to complete his out-landish wardrobe, over his shoulders lay slung a blue cloak with gold trim and white lace at the throat. Strapped to his skinny waist was an ornate curved sword and a brace of flintlocks, and resting on the ground was a rifle.

I was not the only one momentarily dumbfounded, for when I glanced around, I saw that Sergeant Wheatridge and Corporal Fiske were equally astounded. Borke's mouth hung open. Jacob Hyde, though, looked vaguely troubled.

"Greetings, girls!" this apparition cheerfully called out in a voice that crackled like old leather. "If I'd known to expect company, I'd have run some buffalo off a cliff and had your breakfast ready."

Recovering my composure, I rode into the clearing. A saddled horse and a pack animal were tethered nearby. He had been about to leave, I surmised, but heard us coming, and waited. I introduced myself and my sergeant.

"Pleased to make your acquaintance." He rose and smiled, revealing teeth I would not wish on my worst enemy. "Ezriah Hampton is my name, former free trapper and now man of luxury and ease, at your service." Removing his hat, he gave a courtly bow. "How might I be of assistance to a fine band of stalwarts such as yourselves?"

I did not quite know what to make of him. One moment he called us "girls," the next "stalwarts." His attire, and the gleam in his remaining eye, hinted that he might not be in complete possession of all his faculties. But I humored him and said, "I wouldn't mind sharing a cup of your coffee."

"Climb down, climb down!" Hampton urged. "I don't have enough for all of you, I'm afraid. Blame whoever made the coffeepot. If they were big enough and had teats like cows, we could all suck it down at once."

Have you ever heard anything so outrageous? Winking at Sergeant Wheatridge, I dismounted. He and Borke joined me. But not Jacob Hyde, I noticed. "Yes, it would be of great benefit if coffeepots had teats," I agreed with our diminutive host.

Hampton squinted his good eye at me. "Why, that's about the silliest notion I've ever heard. What do they teach you fellers nowadays? Nursery rhymes?"

Now, I ask you, where was the logic in that? "I'm afraid Hansel and Gretel are not part of army training, no," I responded.

Cackling merrily, Hampton clapped me on the arm. "That's the spirit, General! Feed them blood and guts but hold off on the make-believe. Why give them reality when you can drown them in illusion?"

"My proper rank is lieutenant," I reminded him a bit stiffly. He made no sense whatsoever.

Hampton shrugged and filled a battered tin cup. "General, lieutenant, they all shovel manure, when you get right down to it." He held the cup out to me.

I was sure I had been insulted but not quite certain of the context. To stall, I sipped some of his coffee, and I'm here to admit it was some of the most delicious coffee I ever tasted. I complimented him.

"It's my secret ingredient," Hampton said, and tittered.

"What would that be?"

"I piss in it." Cackling louder than ever, Hampton hopped up and down in what I can only guess was his imitation of a jig.

"You are an extremely strange man, Mr. Hampton," I declared.

"The stranger, the better" was his reply. He regarded my men a moment, then the civilians, and finally our scout. "Well, well. Look what crawled out of the salamander's ass."

"I couldn't believe it when I saw you," Jacob Hyde said. "I heard you'd died."

"Ought to clean out your ears now and then," Hampton said. "Might leave room for a brain."

"You two know each other?" I interjected.

Hyde nodded. "It was a long time ago."

"I'll say!" Hampton agreed. "We were younger than you, General. Thought we'd make our fortune in beaver, like John Jacob Astor. But one day we were set upon by Bloods, and this dandelion you're with ran out on me and a couple of others when the arrows were flying thicker than bees around a hive."

"Are you callin' me yellow?" Jacob Hyde demanded, fingering his rifle.

"Do moose farts stink?" was Hampton's rejoinder. He had a hand on one of his flintlocks, and the gleam in his eye was brighter than ever.

"That will be enough, gentlemen," I said. "Mr. Hyde, need I remind you that you are in the employ of the United States Army and subject to my command? And Mr. Hampton, whatever took place between you was decades ago. Surely you can forgive him after all this time?"

"Forgiveness is for cheek-turners, General, and I've only got one peeper left." But Hampton took his hand off his pistol and motioned for me to have a seat. He sank down beside me. "So. What are you girls doing so far from your mommas?"

"I do wish you would stop calling us that. For your information, we are investigating reports of a massacre. Perhaps you're aware that a trading post on the

Green River was attacked and the personnel slaughtered last year?"

Hampton's good eye started to twitch and his smile faded. "Would that be the post on Ham's Fork of the Green?"

I looked at Phineas Borke, who excitedly bobbed his double chin. "Yes! That's exactly where my brother said he planned to build it. Right in the heart of Shoshone country. Have they attacked anyone else since then?"

"The Shoshones?" Hampton snickered. "Hell, they wouldn't attack whites if we were all they had to count coup on." His good eye shifted to me. "I heard the Crows were to blame."

Before I could speak, Jacob Hyde said rather gruffly, "Where did you hear this tall tale, Ezriah?"

"My friends get to call me by my Christian name," Hampton said, "and you ain't one."

I swear, it was ridiculous, these two feisty old men ready to come to blows or worse over an incident that took place long before I was born. "Tell me where you heard the Crows were to blame, if you wouldn't mind."

To my amazement, Hampton reached up and playfully pinched my cheek. "For a girl as pretty as you, Gladys, I'm always eager to oblige."

"My name is not Gladys."

"It should be. But since you asked so pretty, and your nose sort of reminds me of hers, Gladys it is." Hampton's right eye was twitching like mad. "As for where I heard it, it's common knowledge hereabouts."

"Hereabouts?" I repeated. "Can't you be a bit more specific?"

"Oh, between Canaday and Mexipepper."

What was I to make of an absurd assertion like that? His continual play with words was positively aggravating. I truly did begin to think he was insane.

"It's well known those tulips had dealings with the Crows," Hampton said. "Fact is, word has it they were trying to stir up grief between the Crows and the Shoshones to feather their own pockets."

Phineas Borke snapped, "That's a damned lie! Take it back, old man, or so help me, I'll throttle some sense into that scatterbrained head of yours."

"You and what horde of mice?" Hampton did not seem to be the least bit concerned. To me he said, "The Crows are much more likely to kill whites than the Shoshones. Why, the Shoshones haven't harmed so much as a pimple on a white ass since who flung the chunk."

In his bizarre way he had a point. I conceded as much, adding, "You wouldn't happen to know if the trading post is still standing, would you?"

"I can't rightly say. I never went for a look-see, although I reckon I should have. Historical monuments are scarce in these parts."

"I suppose you've never met a man by the name of Nate King, either?" I inquired. Suddenly his right eye stopped twitching and bored into mine. It was several moments before he answered, and I received the impression his comments were guarded.

"Who hasn't? He's about the most famous coon on both sides of the Divide. Up there with Bridger and Carson and Smith and McNair. What's he got to do with the lunkheads who got themselves slaughtered?"

Phineas bristled again. "I'll thank you not to refer to my brother as a lunkhead."

"My mistake," Hampton said, and rephrased his question. "What does Nate King got to do with the shit-for-brains who got themselves rubbed out?"

I set down the tin cup. "You, sir, have a foul mouth."

"That I do," Hampton said, merrily bobbing his chin. "Goes to show what proper rearing will do. But you still haven't told me how this fella King fits into the scheme of creation."

"We've been led to believe that it was his son who led the Shoshones in their attack on the trading post," I detailed.

"Led? By whom? These peckerwoods?" Hampton crooked a finger at Jacob Hyde and Phineas Borke. "Green as you are, Lieutenant, even you must have noticed they're not the most honest babes in the woods. Why, I'd bet my poke you wouldn't invite either home to meet your mother."

There was more to this fellow than I had imagined. One second he spouted lunacies, the next he was as rational as you or I. Note that he called me by my proper rank, and that his observation regarding Borke and Hyde was quite perceptive. I did not let on that I agreed with him, since to do so would antagonize those he had insulted, but I took Hampton more seriously. "Is it your contention, then, that Nate King's son is as highly regarded as his sire?"

"My contention, as you call it, is that the Good Lord has a powerful sense of humor. As for the Kings, I reckon Nate is held in as high regard as any man living, no argument there. His son, folks say, is a tad temperamental, but that's a common failing of the young. Hot blood makes for hot heads."

"Would you happen to know where the Kings live?"

Again his gleaming eye bored into mine. "Hmm. I seem to recollect hearing that they have a cabin somewhere near the Great Salt Lake."

Jacob Hyde muttered something, then said louder, "Don't listen to this old coot, Lieutenant. Nate King has a cabin along the front range. His son, I'm not so sure."

I stood and smoothed my uniform. "You have been most helpful, Mr. Hampton. I thank you for the coffee. But we must be on our way."

Ezriah Hampton's eye was twitching again. "Since you're heading west, I reckon it's only fair to warn you, General. A hostile war party has been roaming these parts the past couple of months, killing red and white alike. Sixty, seventy warriors or more, I hear. Part of the Blackfoot Confederacy. You'd best be mighty careful, or your girls are liable to lose their hair."

He grinned from ear to ear.

# Chapter Five

Rumor is fear's midwife. News of the war party had spread from one end of the column to the other by the time I mounted, and where formerly the men had been in fine spirits, they now envisioned the shadow of death hovering over their heads and became mired in gloom.

I sought to make light of it. We had not gone half a mile when I turned to Sergeant Wheatridge and stated much more loudly than was my wont, "Can you imagine anyone taking what that old man said seriously? For all he knows, those Indians are back in their own territory by now." My hope was that my remark would spread down the line, but if it did, it failed to have the desired effect.

Jacob Hyde did not help matters. Before riding off, he said over his shoulder, "That cantankerous cuss ain't one of my favorite people, but I don't think he was lyin'. Ask me, he's probably hopin' the hostiles will chop us to bits and pieces."

Nothing of note occurred the rest of the day. That evening at the campfire Hyde let it be known that the foothills should be in sight in a few days. Where once smiles and cheers had greeted the news, now it was frowns and frayed nerves. The men were nervous; they talked in low tones, and there was a lot of petty arguing.

I insisted everyone turn in early so we could make an early start. Sergeant Wheatridge suggested that the sentries be doubled, and as an extra precaution, that our horses be hobbled and be kept close at all times.

"I've dealt with the Blackfeet before, sir. There's nothing they like more than stealing horses. Nate King told me they consider it as big a coup as killing an enemy."

The more I heard of this mountain man, the more intrigued I became. What sort of person was he? How was it he had killed so many grizzlies? Why had he given up the white world for the perils of the wild? And what made him want to take a Shoshone as his wife? I doubted I could ever fully comprehend him.

Nate King had done what not one in a thousand would do. No, make that one in ten thousand. Most trappers had gone home after the fur trade collapsed and taken up safer pursuits. Not him. He stayed in the mountains. He braved the daily dangers and carved a niche for himself. What motivated him? The love of a woman? Or was there more to his decision?

What made a man like him do what he did?

I fell asleep without being conscious of drifting off, and the next I knew, a noise brought me instantly awake and I heard Corporal Fiske calling my name and saying, "Indians, Lieutenant! A sentry saw Indians!"

Appearances be damned! I ran from my tent half-dressed, my pistol in hand, to discover the camp seized by frantic commotion. My men were running every which way, some shouting, some pointing, all with their fingers on the triggers of their rifles. "Sergeant Wheatridge?" I bawled. He materialized out of the night, and I was never more thankful for his oaken presence and superb poise. "Deploy the men in a defensive perimeter until we can establish if there is cause for alarm."

Wheatridge was incredible. With a very few commands, articulated loudly but not stridently, he had the camp organized and calm restored. I instructed Corporal Fiske to bring me the sentry who claimed to have seen Indians, and to institute a count of the horses. The count came back complete, and the sentry came shuffling shame-faced at the corporal's heels.

Private Bittles was one of our youngest and newest recruits. This was his first campaign, and he had acquitted himself as well as I could expect. "Sir!" he said, snapping to attention and saluting.

"What is this about hostiles, Private?"

"Three of them, sir. I saw them clear as could be."

The moon was a crescent sliver and the sky smudged by overcast. To say I was not inclined to believe him would be accurate. "You are willing to swear to this?"

"May I be scalped tomorrow if I'm lying, sir."

# David Thompson

Wheatridge had returned and was listening. "Details, Private Bittles. The officer needs details. Brief and to the point, if you please."

"Yes, sir." The young man swallowed. "I have horse duty, sir. I had just come to the end of the string and was turning to come back when I saw them. Three faces peering at me from out of the brush. I immediately gave a shout and raised my rifle to shoot, but they were gone before I could blink."

I glanced at Sergeant Wheatridge, but his expression was hard to read in the dark. Placing my hand on the young recruit's shoulder, I said as kindly as I could, "Think a moment, Private. Isn't it possible your imagination was at work? Or that these faces you think you saw were a trick of light and shadow?"

"As God is my witness, sir, they were real."

I was in a quandary. I did not want to come right out and say the private was wrong, but neither did I want the rest of my men to believe hostiles were spying on us in the dead of night. I turned to Jacob Hyde. "How about it, scout? Isn't it true that Indians are never abroad at night?"

"They generally don't like to attack at night, no," Hyde answered, "but they're sure as hell not scared of the dark. If that war party spotted our fire, I wouldn't put it past them to send a few bucks to count our blankets."

"Count our blankets?" That was a new one on me.

"Count our men," Sergeant Wheatridge clarified. "Indians like to know the strength of their enemies before they attack." He gazed at the many young, pale faces fixed in our direction. "Might I suggest building up our fire, sir? It can't do any harm now."

Not if the hostiles knew we were there, it didn't. "Your request is granted. But have the men turn back in. We need our rest."

It was difficult to get back to sleep. I tossed and turned and sat up at every distant sound. At length I slept, but only for an hour or so, and was up and in uniform at the crack of dawn. I personally woke up each of the men and encouraged them with a smile and a firm grip on the shoulder.

My first cup of coffee helped restore some of my vigor. Whatever other shortcomings Corporal Fiske had, he brewed coffee that would float a horseshoe. As I was scanning the camp, I noticed a conspicuous absence. "Where's our scout?"

"Hyde went to look for sign," Phineas Borke said. "He slipped out before first light so the hostiles wouldn't spot him if they were still watchin' us."

"Why wasn't I consulted beforehand?" I demanded.

"I reckon he didn't think he had to," Borke responded. "And I didn't want to shout for you or do anything to try to stop him that might draw attention."

His explanation was reasonable enough, but no officer likes to have his authority taken so lightly. "The moment he returns, I am to be informed. Is that understood?"

"Sure, sure, Lieutenant, whatever you want. We don't want to step on your toes."

I happened to catch sight of Clemens and Sewell out of the corner of my eye, and damned if they weren't smirking. I was less than amused, and would have spoken my mind had Jacob Hyde not chosen that moment to lope out of the woods. One look at his face and the coffee in my mouth turned bitter.

"The boy was right, Lieutenant. I found three sets of tracks leadin' off to the northwest. Moccasin prints."

"Might they be friendlies?"

"Friendlies wouldn't spy on us in the middle of the night. They'd wait until sunrise and come greet us proper. Besides, no two tribes make their footwear the same. The cut of the soles are always different. These were Piegans, sure as I'm standin' here. And they hate whites somethin' fierce."

There it was. Now all eyes were on me and me alone. The full weight of my command came crushing down on my shoulders as heavily as the weight of the world on the shoulders of Atlas. Although I had long ago mentally accepted the fact that the lives of all these men were in my hands, it was not until this very moment that I felt it, heart, mind, and soul, and I can tell you, it is not a feeling to be courted.

"Well?" Phineas Borke said when I did not say anything soon enough to suit him. "Do we fort up and wait for them to attack?"

"We do not." While the woods were thick and afforded excellent cover, it was not enough to stop a determined foe. I rose to my feet and said to Sergeant Wheatridge, "Prepare to ride out. Since the spies went northwest, it's safe to assume the main body lies in that direction. So we'll ride southwest. With a little luck we can avoid them."

Clemens, who rarely spoke, did so now. "You'd rather run than fight?"

"Our purpose is to investigate the massacre of the trading post staff, not to engage in pointless combat. But rest assured that if we have to fight, we will, and we will do so with distinction."

My men scrambled to break camp. We went without breakfast. Inside of half an hour, we were mounted and ready. I wheeled my horse and rose in the stirrups to address them. "Men of the Second Cavalry. More than ever, from this point on our lives are in our hands. We must be diligent. We must keep our guns loaded, our knives honed sharp. No one is to go off alone. Details will be assigned in pairs. Watch the back of the man next to you, and he will watch yours. We are comrades in arms, gentleman. The army pays us to kill, and before long we might need to earn our keep."

I led them out of the trees and off across open country. I was riding slightly ahead with Sergeant Wheatridge when he made a comment as flattering as it was unexpected.

"If you'll permit me to say so, sir, you have handled yourself extremely well. No officer could do better."

"Does that surprise you, Sergeant?"

"Let's just say, sir, I have seen others behave far less professionally on their first campaign. Colonel Templeton will be impressed."

"He asked you to keep an eye on me, didn't he? No need to pretend otherwise, Sergeant. I can see it in your eyes. And I'm not stupid. He paired us up because you're the best sergeant he has and I was the least experienced. He wanted someone he trusts along to ensure I don't blunder and get us all killed."

Wheatridge indulged in a smile. "You can't hardly blame him, sir, for having the best interests of the men at heart. It's what distinguishes a true officer from those who think only of themselves."

I hadn't ever thought of it that way, and it gave me much to contemplate the rest of the day. We saw no more sign of Indians, hostile or otherwise, although once, about the middle of the afternoon, we spotted a cloud of dust far to the north. It did not come closer and soon was out of sight.

That night we camped in the open. I ordered the fires kept small and had four men guarding the horses at all times. I also set up outposts a hundred yards out in each direction. Shallow trenches were dug for the men lie to in, and they were to fire a shot at the first hint of danger, then fall back on the camp. Everyone was in a state of nervous agitation, and few of us enjoyed a good night's rest. But our worry was for naught.

The next morning dawned bright and clear. I allowed a leisurely breakfast. We took our time saddling up, and the general mood was relaxed and jovial when we headed out. We had not gone far when the western horizon was rimmed by what I took to be clouds, part of an incoming front. But as the hours passed and the clouds came no closer, I realized it was a haze-induced illusion, and that, in truth, I had finally set eyes on the Rocky Mountains. Someone once told me that the highest peaks were visible from a long way off on the prairie, and by the end of the day we could see the tops of dozens.

It meant we were near our destination at long last, and the men bubbled with anticipation. The sooner we reached it, the sooner we could go home, and there wasn't one of us, myself included, who wasn't sick to death of the heat and the dust and the grass and, yes, the smell and sounds of our own horses. We longed for the fort, for civilization, for the little creature comforts we had always taken for granted.

That is often the way, is it not? We don't truly appreciate what we have until we no longer have it. In this respect I was no different from anyone else. The thought made me smile. Why? you ask. Because my wealth and my station in life had always set me apart from ordinary men. When you are rich, others tend to treat you as if you are special. In theory the army had erased that distinction, but only here, in the middle of nowhere, had it truly been obliterated. Other than my rank, I was the same as the rest. We were brothers in spirit as well as in uniform. You cannot fathom how exquisite that feeling was to someone who had always had it pounded into his head that he was better than the common man.

No one should have the right to set themselves above others socially and economically. Therein breeds tyranny. America was founded on the ideal of all men being created equal, and while that certainly was not true in terms of money and luxury, it was true where it counted—in the right to have the opportunity to make of ourselves what we will, without let or hindrance.

Perhaps you think it strange that someone who had lived in the lap of excess should give serious thought to the fount from which that excess sprang. But I tell you here and now that those thus favored, if they have a shred of moral fabric in their soul, often wonder about the rift between those who have a lot and those who have not, and why it should be that anyone should have to go without.

I've strayed from my account. It is hard sometimes to restrict myself to pertinent details when there is so much I want to say. And yet I must, perforce, check my quill pen, for there are only so many pages in this journal, and once I have filled up the last, that is it until I return to Fort Leavenworth and obtain a new one.

Why I bothered at all might puzzle you, but old habits are hard to break and I had been keeping a record of my thoughts and feelings since I was eight years old. To what purpose eluded me, as I never intended for anyone else to read what I wrote. I did it for myself, not anyone else.

But to get back to my narrative, there we were, about five in the afternoon, moving briskly westward, the sun still hours above the horizon, when I spied a lone rider galloping madly toward us. I recognized Jacob Hyde, and seeing his haste, thought it best to bring the column to a halt.

"This does not bode well, sir," Sergeant Wheatridge said.

I fully agreed. I scanned the plain beyond Hyde but saw nothing to account for his urgency. He reined up, wheeled his lathered mount, and pointed. "I saw them miles back. They know right where you are."

I looked again, and there was the dust cloud, as before. But this time it rapidly grew, and soon I could see its source: scores and scores of painted warriors astride their warhorses.

The hostiles were coming to pay their respects.

# Chapter Six

Here again was another of those events difficult to translate onto paper so that full justice is done.

The war party surrounded us, and for over an hour we were subjected to the most horrendous shrieks, whoops, and yells the human throat is capable of making. It was a wonder they didn't wear their throats raw.

Was I afraid? Of course I was. Did I show it? Of course I didn't. We had formed into a circle with our horses in the center, and I strode along the perimeter with my hands clasped behind my back, putting on a show of authority for the benefit of my men. To their credit, they deported themselves well. They were nervous and scared, which was to be expected, but not a man among them succumbed to panic.

I realized that being caught in the open was not the smartest of military tactics. They had us completely hemmed, their line a few warriors deep, enough to warrant that any attempt on our part to break out would be met with the most savage resistance.

Despite the dread they filled me with, I was impressed. Here were true warriors at last. When they weren't screaming and shouting, they conducted themselves with stoic calm. Most were as young as my command. No more than a third of their number, I would hazard, were over thirty years of age, but that is a rough guess, for I am no judge of Indian features and complexion. Still, wrinkles are wrinkles and gray hairs are gray hairs, so by that standard, perhaps my guess was not far off the mark.

At first I thought their screeches and shrieks were a prelude to attack; they were working themselves into a killing frenzy, much as the Viking berserkers of old did. But when some time went by and they had yet to loose a shaft, it struck me that their racket was a form of mental warfare, that it was intended to demoralize and unman us, so when the attack came, they could easily vanquish us.

In any engagement it is always prudent to mark your enemy's leaders. As I walked the perimeter, I sought some clue to the identity of the warrior in charge. Jacob Hyde had told me that while Indians don't conform to the white man's hierarchy of command, extending as it does from the general down to the private, Indians do have a hierarchy of their own.

Ordinary warriors are the equivalent of our privates. But whereas a white man need only enlist and be issued a uniform to become a private, an Indian must count coup or perform some other courageous deed before he is considered a warrior. Those who fail to do so are reduced to the status of women. Warriors of note belong to what Hyde called "societies," groups that police the camps and are always at the forefront of battles. One warrior, and one only, the bravest of them all, is accorded the status of "war chief," which is comparable to a general but with a telling difference. Generals order the men under them around as they see fit; war chiefs have no true authority. They can suggest a course of action, they can offer advice at councils, but they do not have the right to boss others around. War chiefs lead by example. Each warrior then has the right to follow that example or not.

It boils down to every man for himself—an inefficient system, in my estimation, sorely lacking in authority and discipline. Were there ever to come a day when their tactics were pitted against ours in pitched warfare, I was supremely confident that ours would ultimately prevail.

Hyde had informed me that raiding parties such as the one confronting us were usually led by a warrior of note, who proposed the raid to begin with. It was this warrior I searched for, and whom I subsequently found.

It happened thus.

Again and again many of the younger warriors took short running starts toward us, shaking their weapons and whooping, then returned to their line. It was a show of courage, nothing more. One young warrior ran closer to us than the rest, so close that several of my men would have shot him had I not reminded them to hold their fire. The young warrior stood there screeching like a bobcat and taunting us. He was arrogant, this pup, and immensely foolish, and I noticed that when he returned to their line, another warrior came over and spoke sternly to him.

This other warrior was of interest. He was in his forties, possibly, and taller than most. His face bore the stamp of authority typical of a leader, and was painted, like the rest, with lines and symbols that had some special meaning. He had a high forehead and a Roman nose, and carried himself with dignity. A quiver bristling with arrows was slung across his back, and in his left hand was a bow. A knife adorned his waist.

He noticed me staring at him, and for several minutes he took my measure while I took his. Then he tilted his head and gave voice to a yell, and the next instant the hostiles fell silent. Still staring at me, he stepped past their line, slung his bow over his shoulder, and moved his hands and fingers in an exceedingly odd manner.

"It's sign talk," Jacob Hyde said at my elbow. "He's the top dog, and he wants to parley."

"Can you translate?"

"I know sign good enough to get by, but I'm not as fluent as some." The scout gave his rifle to Borke. "We'll have to go unarmed."

I saw the tall warrior give his weapons to another. "Very well." To Sergeant Wheatridge I whispered, "If it proves to be a treacherous trick, avenge me. Drop the leader and the rest might take it as bad medicine and break off." Several weeks ago, during one of our evening talks, Jacob Hyde had mentioned that Indians were big believers in omens, or what they called "medicine." Superstition, to be sure, and one we might exploit.

"I should go with you, sir," Sergeant Wheatridge said.

"Who would lead the troop should both of us be slain?" I shook my head. "No. Mr. Hyde will be sufficient." I straightened my hat and smoothed my uniform and marched toward the tall warrior, my heart doing flip-flops in my chest.

"See those scalps?" Jacob Hyde whispered.

Until that moment I hadn't noticed that some of our swarthy adversaries had what appeared to be fresh scalps hanging from their lances or attached to their person. Indian scalps, from the looks of them.

The tall warrior waited with his arms folded. When we halted, his dark eyes bored deep into mine. After a bit he spoke in hand talk, Hyde translating as the warrior went along. "I am Bear Child of the South Piegans. How are you called?"

Our scout's befuddlement was transparent. "What do I tell him, Lieutenant? It's not like they have signs for Phillip Pickforth."

I wanted something impressive, something that would show Bear Child I was not to be trifled with. "Tell him I'm called Winner of Many Battles."

Hyde's mouth quirked. "Layin' it on a mite thick, aren't you? No disrespect intended, Lieutenant, but I doubt he'd buy it. Not with your baby cheeks."

I would have him explain that last remark later. Right now I said, "Very well. How about something along the lines of Killed Many Men?"

"How about Kills Fast?" Hyde said.

Bear Child digested this much longer than I expected. Then his fingers flew. "I speak as one warrior to another. When will you whites learn you are not welcome in the land west of the Muddy River? We have told your people this many times, but still they come. We have killed many of your kind, but still they come. How long before you stop?" Bear Child lowered his hands, but only for a few seconds. "Whites bring sickness against which we are helpless. We know how it wiped out the Mandans, and we will not let our villages share their fate. That is why I, Bear Child, cannot let any of you leave this spot. That is why all of you will die where you are."

"Is there no reasoning with him?" I asked Hyde.

"You can try. But the Piegans are part of the Blackfoot Confederacy, and you know how they are."

That I did. There were no more implacable whitehaters anywhere. "We'll try anyway. Translate for me." I paused. "I understand that the Piegans do not want whites in their land. I understand that you do not want whites near your villages. But we are not on Piegan land. We are not near a Piegan village. We are on the prairie, minding our own affairs. Just as you should mind yours. For I tell you now that if you raise a war club against us, many of your warriors will die. We have many guns, many bullets. Maybe you will win. Maybe not. It is worth thinking about."

It was a while before Bear Child replied. "Why have you come here, white man?"

"Tell him about the trading post," I directed Hyde.

In due course Bear Child responded. "I have heard of the wooden lodge and the whites who came to trade. I have heard they were wiped out by Crows."

Which was exactly what Ezriah Hampton had claimed, as I recalled.

Bear Child wasn't done. "Now that you know who killed them, I will let you take your men and go. But first you must give your word never to return."

"I thank you for the information, but I cannot leave," I had Hyde sign. "I must see the trading post with my own eyes."

"You will leave, and you will leave now," Bear Child insisted.

We were at an impasse. I had my duty and I would not shirk it. Whether the Piegans liked it or not, we *were* going on, provided we lived, of course. "I have said my final words. I will thank you to move aside so we may pass freely, or the blood of both our peoples will stain this ground red."

I returned to my men and reclaimed my weapons. Bear Child was in heated discussion with five or six members of his war party. All our fates hung on the outcome. I watched intently as their dispute became more and more animated. They were not going to let us depart in peace. I could feel it in my gut. Bloodshed might erupt at any moment. And if it did, if they unleashed sixty or seventy arrows and lances at once, my command would be devastated before we got off a shot.

I could not let that happen.

Whether I was wrong in what I did next, only the Almighty can say. I did what I deemed wisest, and had I to do it over again, I would do the same.

A couple of dozen yards to the north, a handful of warriors had all the Piegan war horses bunched together. If we could drive those horses off, it would strand the Piegans afoot. A sound stratagem any way you looked at it. With that in mind, I whispered urgently to Sergeant Wheatridge, "Spread the word. On my command we will fire a volley into them. Then we will mount up and drive off their animals. Understood?"

"Yes, sir." Wheatridge turned to the men.

Bear Child and the others were still arguing when I gave the order. Sergeant Wheatridge relayed it, ten times louder, and the next moment the air rocked to the thunderous discharge of our rifles. That we took the Piegans by surprise went without saying. More than two dozen dropped where they stood.

It so happened that our enemies had blundered in one respect. When they dismounted and formed their ring, they formed it much too close, well within the effective range of our greenest recruit. Only a few of the Piegans had firearms, old trade rifles, notoriously unreliable, so it's conceivable that they thought they were just out of range when they weren't.

As I intended, our volley blew gaping gaps in their ring. So many rifles, firing simultaneously, resulted in a withering hailstorm of lead. It also resulted in thick clouds of gunsmoke that temporarily hid us and prevented the Piegans from discovering what we were up to. We were astride our horses and in motion in less time than it takes to relate it.

I was in the lead, my saber raised high. When I burst from the smoke, a pair of husky warriors blocked my path, but they did not block it for long. I slashed right and the left, then I was in the clear and racing toward their horses. I was aware of Corporal Fiske on one side of me and Jacob Hyde on the other, and not a sneer between them.

The warriors holding the warhorses reacted quickly. Several swung onto horses, slapped their heels, and were out of there like shots from a cannon. Others notched arrows to the strings of their bows, determined to resist at all costs. At my shout, pistols cracked and their riddled bodies fell, twitching in the throes of their passage into eternity.

We reached the warhorses. Hollering and waving our arms, we incited them to stampede, and soon the majority were in full flight. I looked back but could not see much for the dust and the smoke. "Column west!" I commanded, although technically our formation in no wise resembled one. We galloped pell-mell to put as much distance behind us as we could before the Piegans recovered.

I was proud of myself. My ruse had worked. My men had been delivered from the Piegan death trap, and to my knowledge, we had not sustained a single casualty. I maintained a headlong pace until our mounts had been run to their limit, and if I did not stop, I would do them irreparable harm.

Smiling, I raised my gauntlet and brought my platoon to a stop. "We did it!" I exclaimed.

Borke was as white as paper. "I never want to go through anything like that again!"

"Colonel Templeton should give us all medals," Corporal Fiske cheerfully declared.

That was not apt to happen. Medals must be earned by the most selfless of sacrifices, not deeds performed in the expected course of duty, no matter how daring. "Have the men dismount," I directed. "We will rest fifteen minutes if there is no sign of pursuit."

Just then Private Sawyer came trotting up, so upset he was in tears. "Lieutenant! Come quick! It's Sergeant Wheatridge, sir! He's been hurt!"

Anxiety spiked my chest. It swelled to near-paralyzing fear when I saw the sergeant's large muscular form sprawled in the dust with two arrows jutting from his broad chest. I was off my mount before it stopped moving and knelt beside him, a lump the size of an apple in my throat. It did not stop me from bawling "Get these arrows out!" like an hysterical woman.

Wheatridge's clear blue eyes opened, and he shook his head and placed a big hand on my arm. "They're in too deep, sir. It would do more harm than good."

I refused to accept the evidence of my own eyes. "Lie still. We'll have you on your feet in no time." It was not true, and everyone knew it. Never had I felt so excruciatingly helpless. "How could this happen?" I blurted.

"He was the last one to make a break for it," a trooper said. "He stuck until everyone else was in the clear."

Dear God! What had I done? By rights I should have been last. I was the commanding officer. Wheatridge had done my duty for me. I felt my eyes misting and fought it.

Another soldier was on the ground nearby. Private Bittles, with a broken arrow in his right shoulder.

Sergeant Wheatridge moved his head. "Bittles pulled me out, sir. Came back under a cloud of arrows and got me on his horse. I formally recommend him for the medal of honor. Please do me the courtesy of submitting the paperwork when you get back to Fort Leavenworth."

I could barely talk. "Of course. Is there anything else?"

"No, sir. Thank you, sir." And just like that, Sergeant Wheatridge died.

# Chapter Seven

I passed the next couple of days in an emotional stew. I had lost the best soldier in my command, my right hand, the seasoned veteran whose experience and advice were invaluable. From the outset I had relied on him for everything from tips on how to keep saddle leather from chafing and splitting to how to better motivate the men. Peter Wheatridge had been my rock, my haven, my sanctuary when I was beset by doubts. Now he was gone, and I was to blame.

In my funk I hardly noticed the Rockies increase in size and magnificence until they blotted out half the western sky. Nor was I in any state to appreciate the emerald foothills, arrayed like footstools at the feet of royalty.

The men shared my melancholy. Each and every one had looked up to Sergeant Wheatridge as their ideal of the perfect soldier. More than that, he had always been there for them when they needed advice or a boost in morale. He was friend, mentor, father, brother, all rolled into one.

Not only had the good sergeant been the glue that held our troop together, he was the oil that kept the cogs of our military machine running smoothly. In summation, I can only say that he was the only one among us who was indispensable, so naturally, in a cruel twist of happenstance, fate saw fit to deprive us of him.

Corporal Fiske took it harder than most. Not just because Wheatridge had been his boon companion of several years. With the sergeant gone, Fiske was next under me in the chain of command. He had to assume all of Wheatridge's duties, and the added responsibilities weighed heavily.

Certain members of our party were unaffected by the loss and carried on exactly as before. I am speaking, as you can imagine, of Phineas Borke and his two appendages, Clemens and Sewell, and our scout, Jacob Hyde. To them Wheatridge meant nothing. When we made camp they sat around the campfire joking and laughing as they always did, with no regard for the rest of us. It bred a certain degree of ill will, which, by the way, I shared.

By the third day after the disaster, Borke was in the best mood of our acquaintance, solely because we had reached the foothills and in another few days would arrive at the site of his brother's trading post. It did not help my mood any that he constantly brought up Artemis's death and what he expected to be done about it.

"Yes, sir," he declared as we were winding along. "I can't wait to see the look on Zach King when you take him into custody for my brother's murder."

"First we must conclusively establish that he had a part in the massacre," I said testily.

"We will," Borke predicted. "Just you wait and see." He laughed to himself. "Tell me, Lieutenant. What will the army do to him? Stand him up in front of a firing squad?"

"Military punishments are reserved for military personnel," I mentioned, "and firing squads are reserved for exceptional circumstances. If Zach King is implicated, he will be turned over to the civil authorities and tried for murder."

"What?" The news wasn't to Borke's liking. "Why, that means the Kings can hire a lawyer. And a judge might post bail."

"Zach King will have the same rights as any other suspected criminal, yes," I confirmed. "He's an American citizen, so far as I know, entitled to all the privileges that honor bestows."

Clemens swore under his breath, then said aloud, "Why go to all the bother of draggin' them back to Leavenworth when we can save everyone the expense of a trial?"

"I hope you are not suggesting what I think you are suggesting" was my angry reply. "Need I remind you that my men and I have sworn oaths of allegiance to the United States government and to the Constitution on which that government is based? The military does not have the right to summarily execute citizens."

A retort was on the tip of Clemens's tongue, but he fell quiet at a gesture from Borke, who said, "We would never ask you to do anything, Lieutenant, that goes against the grain of a gentleman such as yourself."

Clemens and Sewell grinned in that sly, devious, belittling way of theirs, and I swear to you, I came close to striking them. But it wouldn't sit well with my superiors, so I contented myself with clucking to my mount and riding on ahead to spare myself their uncouth company.

As I previously noted, the trading post had been built in the vicinity of the Green River, where, it is my understanding, many of the yearly rendezvous were held, back in the days of the fur trade. To reach it we had two routes to choose from. One was to traverse the foothills and cross a series of mountain ranges until we arrived at what has become known as Bridger Basin, wherein the stretch of the Green we wanted is located. The other route was to follow the North Platte River to the Sweetwater and from there cross South Pass and bear west until we struck the Green.

I questioned Jacob Hyde at length about the merits of each. He assured me that water need not be a consideration since he knew all the streams in this region and we would never go without. The second route had more open country to recommend it, which would be less of a trial on my men. But at the same time, in open country we were more likely to be spotted by hostiles, and since Hyde was of the opinion, with which I concurred, that the Piegans were undoubtedly out for revenge, and that by taking the second route we increased the chances of running into Bear Child's war party, I chose the mountainous route.

Once we were in the Rockies, our spirits soared anew. The change from monotonous flat to steep timbered slopes was most welcome until the novelty wore off. We had to contend with one hard climb after another. And if you think riding down a mountain is all that easy compared to going up, then you have never ridden the Rockies, where the slopes are uniformly severe and it takes every iota of horsemanship a rider possesses to spare himself and his mount from harm. After several days we were tired and worn, and I regularly called brief halts to permit our horses to rest.

It was the fourth morning after we left the plains that Jacob Hyde trotted back to report smoke ahead. We proceeded on the assumption that Indians were responsible, and you cannot conceive my wonderment when we came to a ridge that overlooked a beautiful green valley nestled among towering peaks. There, at the valley's center, near a pristine stream, stood a log cabin with tendrils of smoke curling from its stone chimney.

Such a sight in such a setting! It reminded one of home and hearth, and filled me with an intense longing for civilization. I cannot say quite why this should be, unless it was that it touched a nerve deep within me, stirred longings long suppressed. I could tell that many of the men felt the same.

"Have you any idea who lives there?" I asked our scout.

Jacob Hyde's brow was furrowed and he was tugging on his beard, as was his wont when he was deep in thought. He looked at the surrounding mountains, then back at the cabin. "Sure don't. I think it's best we avoid whoever it is and swing around the valley to the north."

He could not have astounded me more if he had claimed the moon was made of moldy cheese. Here was a chance to perhaps learn information crucial to our purpose. Besides, how often did we run into our own kind? In more than a thousand miles the only white man we met was Ezriah Hampton. How marvelous, then, to commune with another, and should the owner prove willing, to spend the night. Fresh companionship would be a treat.

"Don't be ridiculous," I responded. "We're going to pay whoever lives there a visit." I saw Hyde shoot Borke an odd look, so I added, "I want you with us. We'll ride in the open as much as possible on the way down." I did this not only to keep Hyde in my sight but to give the owner of the cabin the courtesy of advance warning of our arrival.

I kept my eyes on the door and the windows, but no one appeared. Several horses were in a corral attached to the cabin, added proof that the occupants were home. Their carelessness appalled me. Had we been a hostile war party instead of a cavalry detachment, they would be overrun and slaughtered.

When we were fifty yards out, I rose in the stirrups and called, "Halloo, the cabin! You have visitors!"

Nothing happened, and I began to wonder if maybe I was wrong and no one was there. Presently I reined up, and I was about to swing down when I was given pause by the click of a gun hammer.

"I wouldn't be hasty there, friend."

I glanced toward the northeast corner and saw a rifle trained on me. At the same instant, the front door opened and the muzzle of another rifle was pointed in our direction. "How do you do, sir," I addressed the speaker, and introduced myself. "With your indulgence, we would like to rest here awhile."

"Would you indeed, sonny?" The speaker stepped into the open. He was as fine an example of a frontiersman as can be envisioned. Clothed in buckskins and moccasins, he was armed with pistols and a knife as well as the Hawken. A powder horn and ammo pouch were slanted across his chest. His hair, like Ezriah Hampton's, was white as driven snow, but where Hampton's had been stringy and sparse, his was thick and lustrous, and his beard neatly trimmed. He grinned, displaying white, healthy teeth, a rarity in someone of his advanced years, for he had to be in his seventies, if not older. Yet you wouldn't know it from the supple grace to his movements, or the vitality in his lively blue eyes.

"I would never presume to impose on your hospitality, sir. Say the word, and my men and I will move on and leave you in peace."

He smiled. "Marry, well said, very well said. Look you, sir. Inquire me first what Danskers are in Pair, and how, and who, what means, and where they keep, what company, at what expense, and finding by this encouragement and drift of question that they do know my son, come you more nearer than your particular demands will touch it." And at that, he performed a courtly bow.

For a moment I thought I was dealing with another raving lunatic like Hampton, perhaps a relation of his, but then he spoke again, to Jacob Hyde and Phineas Borke.

"Welcome, dear Rosencrantz and Guildenstern."

His manner was not nearly as friendly, and I detected a hint of malice in his tone. But the mention of the two gentlemen from *Hamlet* awoke in me the insight that twice now he had quoted the Bard of Avon, in which case he could only be one person. "Shakespeare McNair, I take it?"

"At your service, sir." Again McNair bowed, then stepped to the front door. "It's all right, my fair Juliet. Seal up the mouth of outrage for a while, till we can clear these ambiguities."

Have you ever met a legend? Shakespeare McNair qualified. Long before Bridger, before Carson, before Smith and their ilk, he roved the mountains from end to end. By the time the beaver craze began, he had lived in the Rockies for decades. I am not sure why or where, but somehow he obtained a copy of the works of Shakespeare, and became so versed in the plays and sonnets that he could quote them by the hour. I heard tales of this man when I was a toddler, and here he was, in the flesh, as real as I or my horse. I confess to having been a bit in awe.

"Did you hear me, wench?" he said, and thumped the cabin wall.

The woman who stepped into the sunlight was a full-blooded Indian in a fine buckskin dress. Her oval face bore the stamp of years, although not nearly as many as his, and her long raven hair was sprinkled with gray. What impressed me most was her dignified bearing and her lovely dark brown eyes. She bestowed the most charming smile on me.

Clemens was on my right, and at sight of her, he snorted. "Figures this old buzzard would have himself a squaw."

I could not prevent the next occurrence had I tried. It happened too fast. One instant McNair was standing there calmly and friendly as you please. The next he was beside Clemens's mount and the stock of his Hawken had smashed against Clemens's jaw, spilling him to the ground unconscious.

My men and I were riveted in surprise. Sewell, though, bellowed, "How dare you!" and started to lift his rifle.

In a heartbeat McNair and the woman trained their rifles on him. It sufficed to freeze Sewell as though he were sculpted from ice.

"What here?" McNair quoted. "The portrait of a blinking idiot."

Phineas Borke was squirming in his saddle, he was so mad. "You had no call to do that, mister!"

McNair turned so his Hawken was pointed at Borke. "No one insults my wife. Ever." He nodded at Sewell. "A friend of yours, I take it? Is his head worth a hat? Or his chin worth a beard?"

"What the hell are you babblin' about?" Borke demanded.

"I'll thank you not to swear in the presence of a lady." McNair grinned. "Because the next son of a bitch who does is maggot bait."

Things had gone awfully wrong awfully fast. "Please, Mr. McNair," I interceded. "I find their conduct as deplorable as you do. But I ask you, sir, in the name of civility and decency, not to kill them."

"Civility and decency?" McNair repeated, and winked at his wife. "Now, there's a phrase we don't hear every day, dearest. Very well, Lieutenant. As a personal favor to you, these simpletons can go on breathing. But it's a provisional favor. If they don't mind their manners, they eat lead. Fair enough?"

"More than fair, sir."

The mountain man stared at our scout. "Hyde," he said, as flatly as a slate. Something passed between them, a subtle undercurrent of hostility, I suspected. "Jacob Bartholomew Hyde."

"It's been a spell, McNair. Hard to believe you're still kickin' after all these years. I figured your hair would be hangin' in a lodge somewhere."

"The surprise is mutual," the living legend said. "Justice has been remiss. You deserved to be gutted or hung long ago."

"I didn't know you two knew each other." My confusion was second only to my desire to avoid more trouble. "Might we dismount, Mr. McNair, and see to our horses? I promise we won't be a bother."

"You, sir, are most welcome. The same for the rest of your boys in uniform." McNair swept an arm that encompassed Borke, Sewell, Clemens, and Hyde. "But these four scoundrels are to make their camp at the north end of my valley and stay there until you leave."

"Now, see here!" Borke blustered.

McNair sighted down his Hawken. "It's not open to debate. You have two choices. I'd pick wisely, were I you."

# Chapter Eight

When you are born with a silver spoon in your mouth, as common parlance has it, you dine in the most illustrious of company and under the most illustrious of circumstances. To an extent that is true. I have eaten off the finest of china, drunk from the finest crystal. I have partaken of meals prepared by master chefs. I have supped with senators and bankers, princes and heads of state. Yet never was a meal more enjoyable or the host and hostess more gracious than the evening I shared with the McNairs.

They had sent an invitation to me and as many of my men as I wanted to bring to join them in their cabin for their "evening repast," as Shakespeare referred to it. I took Corporal Fiske along, and that was it. You might think me unkind, but if I had brought others, those left out might harbor resentment.

I do not know what I was expecting when I entered their cabin. Maybe a rustic interior similar to the hunting cabin one of my uncles maintains in upstate New York. You know—a chair or two, a plain table, a bearskin rug, the barest of necessities. But the McNair cabin was much more.

For starters, the floor was covered by a plush rug fashioned from buffalo hides but done in such a clever fashion as to hide the seams and present the illusion that it was one giant hide, not of five or six. Elaborate curtains decorated the windows, each, I later learned, sewn by McNair's wife. As was the rug and the tablecloth and several wall tapestries. The overall impression, in terms of artistry and theme, was a mix of white man and red man presented in a blend extremely pleasing to the eye.

In addition to a dining table there were five straight-backed chairs, a rocking chair next to the hearth, and a settee in a corner. All built by McNair out of oak or pine. His craftsmanship was superb, rivaling that of the best carpenter.

It's the little touches that turn a house into a home, and in this regard our host and his wife were not remiss. There were far too many to relate, from the Flathead knickknacks his wife was partial to, to the large quartz rocks McNair had collected and placed at strategic points around the cabin so they reflected the light, just so, from lamps, not lanterns, purchased by him on one of his periodic jaunts to St. Louis.

Blue Water Woman had changed into a fetching white buckskin dress decorated with the most artful design of beads and small stones in rainbow hues. A more gracious individual you could not hope to meet. Not once did I detect a hint of unladylike behavior. I daresay she could hold her own at any blue-blood social function.

I also discovered, much to my delight, that she was fluent in English. So much so, I would swear she had been raised white. When I lavished praise on her, she smiled ever so sweetly.

"If you think my English is adequate, you should hear my good friend Winona King. She puts me to shame."

"You know the Kings, then?" I asked.

Shakespeare laughed lightly. "I should hope to heaven we do. Nate is the son I never had, and hardly a month goes by I don't see him or his boy, Zach. They're my nearest neighbors."

Here indeed was a stroke of luck, and in my excitement I almost blurted out the charge laid against the Kings by Phineas Borke. It would be an unforgivable blunder, since my host was hardly likely to supply the information I needed if he suspected the reason I needed it.

I was saved by Blue Water Woman, who came to the table bearing the first of a dozen mouthwatering dishes. She had prepared a feast. Just the day before, her husband had shot an elk, and that smoke we saw curling from their chimney was from the fire under a huge pot of stew simmering on a tripod in the fireplace. We also had thick, juicy elk steak, thin strips of elk meat flavored with salt and crushed berries, potatoes smeared in butter, an excellent pudding the likes of which I had never savored, ample portions of beans, and piping hot bread. For dessert we were treated to a slice of berry pie.

Lest anyone think poorly of me for wallowing in culinary heaven while my men had to make do with beans and hardtack, be it noted the McNairs insisted on sharing their stew with everyone, and they would not sit down to table until each man had brought his mess kit to their door and had his tin plate heaped high.

They were generous and kind to a fault, this frontiersman and his wife. Which explains my twinge of conscience after our meal concluded and we sat back to smoke our pipes. I did not go at the subject uppermost on my mind directly, but began my foray with "Doesn't it ever get lonely, just the two of you out here all by yourselves?"

McNair patted his wife's hand and smiled. "Sometimes one person is all the company you need. Besides, we have plenty of visitors. The Kings stop by regularly, as do other settlers. Then there's my wife's kin, who swing by whenever they're in our neck of the woods."

"That's right," I said as casually as I could. "You mentioned something earlier about Nate King and his son. I've heard of them."

"They're as fine as fine gets," McNair said with great affection. "There isn't a coon in these mountains who doesn't think highly of Nate."

"Is his son as widely respected?" I inquired.

"Zach? He's not quite the man his father is, but he's still young. Give him a few years to make his mark and his steel will temper true." McNair fished a lucifer from a pouch at his side.

"I seem to recall you saying the Kings are your neighbors. But I didn't see any other cabins on our way in."

McNair had a hearty laugh that he indulged in often. "I should hope not! As much as I like them, a man needs elbow room. Zach lives a couple valleys to the south, Nate past him a piece."

I was about to ask for precise directions when Corporal Fiske spoiled everything by speaking out of turn.

"Pardon me, Mr. McNair, but do you think Zachary King had anything to do with the massacre we're here to investigate?"

I could have punched him. Sergeant Wheatridge would never have made a mistake like that. I saw alarm flick from husband to wife, and a new, guarded expression came over McNair.

"What is this nonsense?" The mountain man gave me a pointed look. "Strange you didn't mention it sooner."

"It's probably nothing," I said with a shrug. "A vague rumor connecting the Kings to the disappearance of some traders."

Corporal Fiske compounded his blunder by saying, "The brother of one of the missing men lodged a complaint. Phineas Borke. You met him when we arrived. The heavyset gentleman."

"He claims the Kings were involved?" Shakespeare McNair snorted. "That's ridiculous. Everyone in these parts knows the Crows were to blame."

This made three assertions to that effect. "Were you actually present when the massacre occurred?" I asked.

68

"Can't say as I was, no. All I've got to go on is hearsay and the evidence at the scene."

"You've been there?"

"About three weeks after it happened, as I recollect. Some of my wife's people got wind of it and told me. There wasn't much left of the bodies. But I saw five or six arrows the Crows left behind, and more Crow tracks than you can shake a witch's cauldron at."

"Do you give me your solemn word the Crows were to blame?" Part of his legend had to do with his reputation for being as honest as George Washington. Which made his answer all the more disheartening.

McNair's mouth twisted in a lopsided grin, and he quoted, "I am a very foolish fond old man, fourscore and upward, not an hour more nor less. And, to deal plainly, I fear I am not in my perfect mind." He paused. "To that extent, yes, you have my word."

The wonderful warm feeling that had filled me all evening was snuffed out like the flame of a candle smothered by a chill wind. "In that case," I held up my end of the farce, "there can be no doubt. But I am still obligated to visit the site. Perhaps you would be so kind as to provide directions?"

For another hour we indulged in idle talk, but my heart was not in it. I thought the matter dropped and was about to ask them to excuse us so we could turn in when McNair brought it up again on his own accord.

"If I can be of any help in your investigation, just ask. I don't know much, other than that the traders were up to no good and got what was coming to them."

In for an inch, in for a mile. "No good in what respect?"

"Borke's brother was here to trade. He and his men were after gold, and hoped to trick the local tribes into revealing where they could find it. To that end, and to compound their villainy, they sold whiskey after promising the Shoshones not to." McNair forgot himself and growled, "I'd have killed them myself once I found out."

"That's called murder, Mr. McNair. And in case your long stay in these mountains has dulled your memory, it's frowned on."

"East of the Mississippi that's true. But out here, what you call murder we call protecting the lives of our loved ones and preserving our hides. You can't judge our world by yours, Lieutenant."

"In both worlds American citizens are entitled to the full protection of the law," I reminded him.

McNair sighed and set his pipe down. "I suppose I shouldn't be surprised. This was bound to happen eventually. Purgatory has come to Paradise and it will never be the same."

"You've lost me," I admitted.

"Do you know what freedom is, Lieutenant?"

"You ask that of someone who has enlisted in the service of his country to keep this great nation of ours free for all?" True, I had other reasons for joining, but no one could fault me for failing to live up to my responsibilities as an American. "Freedom is the right to do as a person desires so long as those desires do not violate the common good."

"That's a pretty fair definition," McNair allowed. "But that's civilized freedom, not the true kind."

"There's a difference?"

"The difference between a wolf running wild and a pet wolf on a leash. Out here a man and woman can do as they full well please without anyone looking

70

over their shoulders to say what is wrong and what is right. Out here we're answerable to no one but ourselves, and if we step over the line, we pay the price. In the States people are under the rule of law. What they can do, and what they can't, is dictated by those who hold their leashes."

I had never heard freedom described in quite these terms before. "Rather a quaint and naive notion, don't you think? Granted, laws nibble away at our free will. But they're essential. Without them, chaos would reign."

"We don't have laws out here, yet we manage to get by," McNair countered. "True freedom is Paradise, Lieutenant. It's the closest state to heaven on earth. Once laws are introduced, once a few can impose their views on how a man should behave by etching their views in legal stone, true freedom becomes a thing of the past." He smiled rather sadly. "You, sir, are a harbinger of the beginning of the end. Until now we have always been left to deal with our problems as we've seen fit."

"You would have the United States overlook a massacre of its citizens? The government has a responsibility to those who support it to see that those responsible for such atrocities are severely punished."

Again McNair and Blue Water Woman shared glances. "And what if you find that those responsible were justified? That Borke's brother and the others were as vile as I've painted them? Will you let those who did it off the hook?"

"That would be presumptuous of me. Judgment and justice are the province of our legal system. I'm a simple soldier. My function is to find out who was to blame and take them back to stand trial."

"No bending of the rules for the sake of what is right?"

"Bend a rule once and it becomes a habit. Before long, all rules are worthless." I shook my head. "No, my duty is clear, and I intend to carry it out to the fullest of my ability."

"I commend your diligence, if not your outlook" was McNair's troubled reply. Then he quoted the Bard again, more to himself than to me: "Are you called forth from out a world of men to slay the innocent?"

For a short while more we discussed trivial things like the weather, then I rose and thanked them for a wonderful evening.

"Mighty fine folks," Corporal Fiske commented as we strolled toward my tent.

I was still annoyed at him for his blunder, but I was too preoccupied with the implications of my talk with McNair to take him to task. Sleep was a long time coming. My mind would not rest. I explored the problem from every angle and always came back to the same staring point.

The next morning I was one of the first up. The sun had not yet risen, but a pink glow suffused the eastern sky. I walked to the stream to wash and was startled out of my lethargy by a figure who materialized from out of the shadows.

"Good morning," Shakespeare McNair greeted me. He had been seated on a tree stump, as if waiting.

"You're an early riser, I see," I said to cover my embarrassment.

"When you reach my age, Lieutenant, time becomes precious. Every minute squandered is a minute that could be spent living life to the fullest." He did as he was famed for doing. "What is a man, if his chief good and market of his time be but to sleep and feed? A beast, and no more. Surely, he that made us with such large discourse, looking before and after, gave us not that capability and godlike reason to fust in us unused."

"I hope I have half your wisdom when I'm your age," I complimented him. I was sincere. I respected him greatly.

"Think me wise, do you?" McNair made sure none of my men were nearby. "In that case, mark my words. No good can come of this mission of yours. Do everyone in these parts a favor and head back."

I would have liked nothing better than to accommodate him. I have many faults, but being a fool is not one of them. "I can't do that. I'm sorry."

"So am I, Lieutenant Pickforth. So am I."

# Chapter Nine

Phineas Borke had no more than a general idea of the location of his brother's trading post. We searched for five days without finding it; our failure was due in part to the fact that we were acting under the assumption the trading post still existed. In our ignorance we rode past it twice, within a few hundred yards, without realizing how close we were.

The sixth morning I sent a detail to a ridge to reconnoiter, and they returned in great haste to bid me see what they had seen.

The trading post had been burned to the ground and was now partly overgrown with weeds and grass. It had stood near Ham's Fork of the Green River, all right, in as perfect a spot as anyone could want. From the charred ruins I determined that the traders had built themselves a palisade, a prudent precaution, as well as a number of buildings besides the trading post proper. Their industry suggested that they intended to stay a good long while.

We found a number of arrows, some broken, some intact. When I showed them to Jacob Hyde, he claimed he could not tell whether they were Crow or Shoshone. This was the same man who could differentiate Blackfoot tracks by the cut of their moccasins.

Private Bittles was poking at the rubble with the toe of a boot and dislodged a piece of timber. "Lieutenant!" he exclaimed. "You'd best come have a look!"

He had found a human skull. Subsequent searching uncovered half a dozen skeletons, some complete, some partial. Bullet and arrow holes and the marks of edged weapons testified to their violent deaths.

"Were they all white?" Corporal Fiske wondered.

I was not expert enough to say for certain, but I couldn't see Indians leaving their dead behind. I picked up one of the skulls. The bone split from above the brow to below the nasal passages, the handiwork of a tomahawk, unless I was mistaken. All the evidence pointed to hostiles.

Phineas Borke was in a daze. He had known his brother was dead, but finding the ruins made it that much more real, and his loss that much harder to bear. "I told Artemis this was a bad idea," he said as he held the same skull I had examined. "But he always was a stubborn cuss."

Clemens and Sewell were nosing around the debris. They were hunting for something and trying hard not to be obvious about it but failing miserably. Whenever

I walked anywhere near them, they promptly moved to a different spot.

"Orders, sir?" Corporal Fiske asked after we had been there an hour.

"Assemble a burial detail. Have graves dug on the hill to the northeast. We'll camp here the rest of the day and head out in the morning."

"Head where, sir, if you don't mind my asking?"

That was the question. I mulled it over long and hard and made my decision before turning in. It was imperative we locate the homesteads of Zach and Nate King and question them. It was not necessarily something I wanted to do but something I had to do if I ever wanted to look at my reflection in a mirror again.

The next day we had been under way a couple of hours when one of the men hollered and pointed. A large group of mounted Indians were shadowing us atop a rise. I immediately had the men take up a defensible position in a stand of aspen.

The Indians made no attempt to thwart us. Shortly after we were dug in, Corporal Fiske called my attention to two warriors descending toward us. Both carried lances and bows and had quivers slung across their backs. When they were fifty yards out, they embedded their lances in the ground and came on with their arms stretched out from their sides to show that their intentions were peaceful.

Handing my rifle to a private, I ordered Corporal Fiske to do the same. Together, we walked out to meet the envoys. One of the warriors was far bigger than the other, but I had no true conception of exactly how big until we halted in front of them. Quite simply, he was the largest man I had ever met. A giant, a Goliath in beaded buckskins, who smiled and said something in his native language.

"How will we understand them?" Corporal Fiske whispered.

Jacob Hyde was off scouting the lay of the land. Without him, any hope of communicating with them was a vain one. I did not know sign, and their dialect was so much gibberish.

Then the other warrior smiled and said in slightly accented English, "Our leader welcomes you. Our people, the Shoshones, have long been friendly to white men."

"How is it you know English?"

"I learned your tongue from Grizzly Killer. Among your kind he is called Nate King." The warrior touched his chest. "I am Drags the Rope. This is Touch the Clouds."

I told them who I was. The giant dismounted, came over, and placed hands as big around as my hat on my shoulders. His smile was friendly, I'll grant him that. Drags the Rope relayed his words.

"You and your men will not be harmed so long as you are in our country. On this you have my promise."

"I thank you," I responded. "We are only passing through and will soon be gone."

Touch the Clouds gazed toward the aspens. "We do not often see blue coats. We would be honored if you will visit our village and sit with us in council."

I debated whether to accept. No matter how friendly the Shoshones were reputed to be, my men did not hold Indians in a flattering regard. Placing them in close proximity might be asking for grief. "I am sorry, but our business is urgent and we must be on our way."

"What business is that?"

I could have lied. I could concoct any excuse. But an inner voice warned me not to. They were probably aware of our visit to the ruins. They might also be aware of our stay at McNair's. Better, then, to be forthright than to arouse suspicion. "We are investigating the deaths of the whites from the trading post."

"They were bad men," Drags the Rope translated. "They spoke with two tongues, and brought much trouble on my people."

"Did the Shoshones wipe them out?" I bluntly demanded.

Touch the Clouds removed his hands from my shoulders and stepped back. "Shoshones do not kill whites."

It was not the answer I wanted. I pointed at his quiver and asked, "Do you mind if I take a look at one of your arrows?" To Corporal Fiske I said, "Run and fetch the arrows we found at the site. I want to compare them."

They were completely different. Oh, they had feathers and barbed points, but there the similarity ended. The Shoshone arrow was a hand's width longer, the fletching was smaller, the tips weren't shaped the same. I asked to see one of Drags the Rope's arrows and his was almost identical to Touch the Clouds's. Quite clearly, the arrows we had found were not Shoshone arrows. Thanking them, I handed the two shafts back.

"We insist you visit our village," Touch the Clouds unexpectedly said.

I had made my position plain and repeated the need for us to move on.

"It is important," Touch the Clouds relayed through his companion. "Very important. One night is all I ask."

I glanced at the fifty to sixty warriors on the rise. Despite the tribe's vaunted friendliness, I didn't care to antagonize them. "How long would it take to get there?"

"That long." Touch the Clouds pointed at a point in the sky corresponding to one o'clock in the afternoon. Their village couldn't be far.

"Do we dare trust them, sir?" Corporal Fiske asked.

I suppressed a scowl. He had done it with Drags the Rope right there. If I refused, the Shoshones would regard it as an insult, and I can't say as I'd blame them. "Everyone speaks highly of your people," I told Touch the Clouds. "I do not have time to spare, but I will make an exception in your case. We would be honored to spend the night with your people."

Imagine what it would be like to be surrounded by wolves and escorted to their den, and you have a fair idea of how I felt as the Shoshones ushered us north along the Green River to their encampment. The only Indian villages I had seen so far were the wretched hovels of the Kanzas and the deer hide huts of the Otoes, and I wondered how the Shoshones would fare by comparison.

My initial impression was of elegant simplicity. They arranged their lodges in great circles, with the flaps, or entrances, facing east, the significance of which eluded me. Almost all the lodges bore painted symbols. Their design was ingenuous, consisting of buffalo hides supported by long slender poles. They varied in size, due, I later learned, to the relative wealth of the occupants. That's right. They had "rich" and "poor" Indians, just as we have rich and poor whites, and those at the lower end of the spectrum had the smallest lodges and the fewest horses.

Did I mention those horses yet? Horses were their currency, their gold, a measure of their status. The village contained no more than two hundred and fifty Shoshones, but their horses numbered in the thousands. Small boys guarded the herds within sight of the encampment.

Everyone flocked out to greet us, and I do mean everyone. Every last warrior, woman, and child. These were not dirty, half-starved scarecrows. The men were strapping specimens. The women were not what I would call beautiful by white standards but were attractive nonetheless. And the children were like children everywhere: inquisitive, playful bundles of energy.

Their friendliness was undeniable. I did not see one hostile face upturned to us as we rode in. I saw smiles, lots of smiles, and heard warm words of welcome whose meaning was conveyed by their expressions.

My men deported themselves in a manner befitting soldiers. They sat straight and tall in the saddle, and when we wheeled into the circle and drew rein, they did so with the crisp efficiency of a unit on parade. I had them stand at attention a good ten minutes to impress the Shoshones with our bearing and our discipline. Whether it worked or not, I cannot say. I do know the Shoshones showed us great respect and courtesy.

Touch the Clouds and Drags the Rope were giving me a tour of the village when I set to prying information out of them. "You mentioned Nate King earlier. I've heard of him. Do you know him well?"

"We call him Grizzly Killer," the giant answered. "Many winters ago he was adopted into our tribe. We regard him as one of our own."

"He has a Shoshone wife, doesn't he?" I feigned ignorance.

"Winona. She and I are cousins," Touch the Clouds revealed. "They have two children, Stalking Coyote and Blue Flower. Or, as you would call them, Zach and Evelyn."

"Is the son a chip off the old block?" I asked, and when they did not understand, I rephrased it. "Does the son follow in his father's footsteps?"

"Stalking Coyote is much like Grizzly Killer. He is very strong, very brave. And he never turns his back on his mother's people."

"So if the Shoshones were in trouble, Zach King would come to their aid?"

"Yes," Touch the Clouds answered without hesitation. "I am proud to call him my friend."

I pointed at Borke, Clemens, and Sewell. "See those whites? They say it wasn't Crows who wiped out the traders. They say Zach King had a hand in it, and the Shoshones helped." I had played my trump card to gauge their reaction, and it was everything I had hoped.

Touch the Clouds stopped in midstride and glanced sharply at me, then leaned toward Drags the Rope and whispered something in their language.

"He says he will forgive your insult but you must not accuse us again. We have brought you here to show you we spoke with a straight tongue when we told you our people can be trusted."

"I have no doubt of that," I said glibly, and permitted them to guide me into the largest lodge. You would not think, to look at them from the outside, how spacious they are. The women stayed to one side, while the men sat in a semicircle in the center. Only older warriors were present; the rest had to stand outside.

"We will smoke the pipe of peace," Drags the Rope informed me.

Indians place a lot of stock in ceremony, so I decided to go along with their wishes for the time being. I am not a smoker and never have been, so I am afraid I coughed and hacked when my turn came, much to their amusement.

It is often said that whites and Indians are nothing alike, but I can say with the authority of firsthand knowledge that they are more like us than you may think. They smile. They jest. They laugh. They talk up a storm at their councils, exactly like certain politicians I can think of. Their most esteemed warriors each gave a speech reaffirming the bond between their people and ours.

Drags the Rope droned on and on, translating, the particulars. One oration tended to blend into the next, and between that and the heat, it was all I could do to keep from dozing off. But it is amazing what you can accomplish when you put your mind to it, or must be on your guard against possible treachery by scores of heavily armed warriors.

You might think ill of me, but I didn't fully trust them. How could I, when I had yet to establish their innocence with regard to the massacre? Only a fool lets down his guard when he is invited into a wolf's lair.

I was expected to give a speech. I limited myself to a few brief statements about how happy the White Father in Washington would be when he heard about our kindly reception. I also stressed that the key to continued peace between our two peoples depended on the Shoshones always being truthful and sincere.

This met with more than a few averted faces. They had no more guile than children, these Shoshones, when it came to hiding secrets.

Last to make an address was Touch the Clouds. It was more of the same until the end, when he looked directly at me and said through his interpreter, "Yes, my people and yours have long seen through the same eyes. Yes, we have been proud to call the white man our brother. But that could change if the White Father does not respect our wishes and leave that which has happened for us to work out."

Was it me, or had he just issued a threat?

# Chapter Ten

True to their reputation, the Shoshones had treated us kindly, but under the surface lurked a current of apprehension. They did not want us prying into the trading post massacre. Several times I tried to draw Touch the Clouds into a discussion about it, but the most he would commit himself was to say the traders had been "bad men" and it was a good thing they had been slain.

They insisted we pitch camp in the center of a great circle. For our protection, Drags the Rope told me. But we were surrounded by lodges, and the thought of all those warriors resenting our presence was enough to make my rest extremely fitful.

Small wonder, then, I was up at the crack of dawn. I had not undressed the night before, so all I had to do was jam my hat on my head and step out into the crisp chill of the morning air. I stretched, admired the remaining stars, then stepped to where our fire had been with an eye to rekindling it so I could enjoy a cup or two of coffee.

To the west, a horse herd milled about as if the animals were restless. I did not think much of it and squatted to select kindling from a pile my men had gathered the night previous. It was so quiet, so still, that the shuffling tread of someone approaching the circle reached my ears. I looked, and there was a dark figure weaving as if intoxicated. It stumbled and tripped and pitched to the ground, and I heard a groan.

My first impulse was to give a general alarm. But that would wake the Shoshones, and they might not take kindly to having their slumber disturbed. Drawing my pistol, I went to confirm my hunch.

The figure was crawling toward the lodges. I realized it was one of the boys assigned to guard the herds, and I sank to one knee and put a hand on his arm. He jerked back when I touched him, then saw me and tried to speak, but all that came from his mouth was blood. Only then did I see the wound. He had been stabbed in the left side. Gritting his teeth, he raised himself on an elbow and with his other arm pointed at Touch the Clouds's lodge and said something in Shoshone.

I did not understand the words, but his message was plain. As I ran toward it, I glanced at the horses and saw they were more agitated then ever. Among them flitted two-legged shapes.

Have you ever tried to knock on a tepee flap? I smacked it several times as hard as I could and called out urgently, "Touch the Clouds! Quickly, man! It's Lieutenant Pickforth."

The flap was flung aside, and he poked his head out. He was dressed in a breechcloth, nothing more, and even bent over as he was, he was huge. His face screwed up in a quizzical question mark, and I pointed at the boy and urged, "Come! Come!"

Once Touch the Clouds noticed the small prone form, he reached the boy in several long bounds and scooped him into his arms. The boy croaked a few words and went limp. Touch the Clouds spun toward the herds, recognized the scope of the crisis, and throwing back his head, gave voice to what I can only describe as a keening yip. A signal, evidently, for hardly had it faded when lodge flaps all around the circle began opening and warriors burst out, most partially dressed but fully armed.

Touch the Clouds ran to his own lodge and ducked inside with the boy. He was in there barely twenty seconds. When he reappeared, he had his bow and arrow and a knife at his hip.

The warriors converged on their leader, and at a whoop from him, they streamed toward the horses. They seemed to have forgotten me and my men, since no one thought to enlist our assistance. I ran to the center of the circle, where, for once, Corporal Fiske was doing something right; he was rolling everyone out of their blankets and forming them up to ward off an attack.

"What is it, sir?" the corporal asked between shouts. "Are the Shoshones fixing to do us in?"

"Their village is being raided," I enlightened him. "Someone is after their horses." It could be any one of a dozen tribes: the Crows, the Sioux, the Cheyenne, or others. Such raids were common, with each spawning a reprisal in an unending cycle.

"What do we do, sir?"

I was wondering exactly that. Colonel Templeton had stressed that I was to avoid conflict with Indians as much as possible, and to never engage in combat unless to defend ourselves. I was to "remain neutral towards all," were his exact words. But the Shoshones were friendlies. And the image of the young boy with blood gushing from his mouth did not sit well with me.

Accordingly, I led my men on foot toward the heart of the commotion, leaving four troopers behind to watch over our animals.

Everyone in the village was astir by now. Most of the warriors had gone with Touch the Clouds, but enough remained to guard against a flanking maneuver. I was surprised to find that almost all the women were armed and, by their attitude and stance, fully prepared to sell their lives dearly in the defense of their loved ones.

The sun had risen. Its spreading glow revealed a huge cloud of dust where the horses should be. I caught glimpses of warriors darting hither and fro, attended by a chorus of whoops and shrieks. But I could not make sense of who was doing what, and indeed, could not tell friend from potential foe.

I brought my men to a halt. All we could do was wait as the light brightened and the dust grew and the sounds of conflict drifted to the northwest.

Presently, from out of the dust sprinted Drags the Rope. He was naked from the waist up, and in his right hand he clutched a war club smeared scarlet. He was making toward the lodges, but when he spotted us he veered in my direction.

"Who has attacked you?" I inquired. "How fares the battle?"

"Piegans!" he spat. "They killed our horse guards. We have caught them, but they will die hard." He hurried on.

I debated what to do. The Shoshones had things well in hand, apparently, and did not need our help. There was nothing to stop us from leaving as I originally intended. But I could not help being curious. Here was a rare opportunity to observe Indians at war, something few whites had ever witnessed.

"Do we head out, sir?" Fiske asked.

"We do not." I wheeled them and double-timed to our horses. Fortunately, we had tethered our animals in the circle with us or the Piegans might have tried to steal them, as well. We wasted no time saddling up, and in short order I was at the head of the column, trotting to where the Shoshones had the raiders at bay.

I will describe the scene in particular detail so its uniqueness may be better appreciated.

Not quite half a mile from the village reared what was left of a small bluff. Long ago, a natural upheaval had caused part of it to collapse, leaving a three-sided horseshoe of perhaps an acre, with walls thirty feet high. Into this the raiders had retreated. The high earthen walls offered as much protection as a palisade, and were so steep that the only way the Shoshones could get at the Piegans was through the mouth of the horseshoe, which was littered with boulders behind which the raiders had secreted themselves.

The Shoshones had the bluff surrounded and were content for the moment to wait for reinforcements. Soon hundreds were present, and the leaders called a council to decide on the best course of action.

"Look there, sir!" Corporal Fiske declared, pointing.

A tall Piegan had climbed onto a boulder to survey the situation, heedless of the risk to his person from bullet and arrow. It was our old acquaintance, Bear Child. He noticed us and raised an arm, but whether in salute or derision, I cannot say. We were sixty yards southeast of the bluff, well out of harm's way but in an ideal position to view all that transpired.

The racket the Shoshones made was deafening. Everyone, from oldest to youngest, male and female, screeched and screamed like banshees, the better, I suppose, to instill fear into their adversaries. But if Bear Child was any indication, the Piegans regarded the Shoshones with ill-concealed contempt.

"Do you think that bunch will surrender, sir?" a private piped up.

"If they don't, they'll be wiped out," another commented.

"They'll be wiped out anyway" was the opinion of a third. "I've heard Indians never let an enemy live."

"They take women and children captive sometimes," the first one remarked.

"Quiet," I said, to instill discipline. I had them dismount and bid them be at ease, then I roosted on a convenient log to await developments.

Corporal Fiske stayed by my side. "Here comes that one who can speak English, Lieutenant."

Drags the Rope was flushed with excitement. "I bring word from Touch the Clouds. He is sorry. But he says this is a Shoshone matter. We must deal with this ourselves."

"I fully agree," I assured him.

"No matter what?"

"No matter what," I reiterated.

"It will not be—" Drags the Rope hesitated, as if seeking the right word, and the one he chose almost made me laugh: "pretty."

"We are grown men. Nothing that happens will upset us."

"You are sure?"

I was perplexed by his insistence. "You have my word as an officer and a gentleman that we will not interfere. Go back to Touch the Clouds and tell him he is free to do as he pleases."

Drags the Rope clapped my arm and ran off. A few shots had been fired at the Piegans by the few Shoshones who owned rifles, but the raiders were too well entrenched, and as near as I could tell, it was a waste of lead.

The screaming and keening died down and I saw the Shoshones prepare to attack. They formed into a large body, thirty or forty warriors abreast. With Touch the Clouds at the forefront, they advanced up a short incline to the mouth of the horseshoe, where they were met by dozens of arrows. Quite a few were felled. Then they were in the opening, but it was so narrow that only half a dozen could engage the Piegans at any one time. The fight was fierce and heated. After a few minutes the Shoshones broke off and retreated, the taunts and hoots of the Piegans heaping shame on top of injury.

I could not fathom why the Shoshones had given up so easily until I saw several warriors supporting Touch the Clouds.

"They'll take that as a bad omen," Jacob Hyde said.

I had forgotten about the scout and the civilians. They were crouched nearby, as fascinated as the rest of us. "Do you honestly think the Piegans stand a prayer?" I asked.

"It depends on how long they can hold out and how many Shoshones they can kill," Hyde answered. "Indians don't like to lose a lot of their own. If a fight is going against them, they'd rather live to fight another day than die for no reason."

Another foray was hastily organized. I did not see Touch the Clouds among the Shoshones. Again their warriors surged into the pocket; again the Piegans repulsed them after a savage contest of arms and wills. Shoshone dead and wounded were carried back and another council was held. In the meantime, women moved among the warriors, passing around water skins and distributing food.

It occurred to me that all the Shoshones had to do was starve their enemies out. Seven or eight days without food and water, and the Piegans would be too weak to offer much resistance. I mentioned this to Jacob Hyde.

"They could do it, all right, but they won't. The Shoshones pride themselves on being warriors, and warriors would never do anything that cowardly."

An hour went by. The Piegans continued to shout taunts and insults, but the Shoshones did not rise to the bait. Touch the Clouds reappeared, his side bandaged. He roved among his people, encouraging them. After a while he came toward us, Drags the Rope and several others in tow.

"I am glad you were not gravely hurt," I said by way of greeting. "Those Piegans mean business."

"One of my ribs deflected an arrow," Touch the Clouds said through his friend. "A little lower and I would not be standing here."

"Those are the same Piegans I told you about last night. The ones who caught us on the prairie."

"They will never bother your kind or my people ever again after we are finished with them," Touch the Clouds predicted.

"Do you ever show mercy to your enemies?" I wondered. An instructor of mine at West Point believed mercy was the one quality that most set us apart from the lower orders.

"We show them the same mercy they show us. To do otherwise would make them think we are weak, and weak tribes are driven from their land and forced to live where there is not much game or water. Or they are wiped out."

I thought of the Kanzas and the Otoes. "What would happen if you asked the Piegans to surrender?"

"They would think we insulted them. And they would laugh at us." Touch the Clouds grew somber. "The Piegans will fight us to the last warrior, as they must."

"Taking a lot of yours with them."

"It cannot be helped. We must show them we are not afraid. Otherwise we shame ourselves in their eyes and our own." Touch the Clouds turned to go, then paused. "Death is as much a part of our lives as life. Each of us knows one day we might need to die for the welfare of our tribe."

"How often does something like this happen?"

"Too often. The last time it was the Crows. The bad whites at the trading post turned them against us and much blood was spilled." He would have said more about the traders, I imagine, but a shout sent him hastening to his people. They were about to try once again to vanquish the Piegans.

"The nerve of that heathen," Phineas Borke commented. "Injuns have been killin' Injuns for as long as anyone can remember, but he tries to pin the blame for their fracas with the Crows on my brother. How stupid does he think we are?"

I could not answer for Touch the Clouds, and I would not answer for myself. At any rate, I was more interested in the next phase of the clash, which was about to commence.

Call me coldhearted, but I found this more entertaining than a night at the opera.

# Chapter Eleven

Up until now, despite being greatly outnumbered, the Piegans had done a remarkable job of keeping the Shoshones at bay. The terrain worked in their favor. The narrow bottleneck and the nearly sheer slopes prevented the Shoshones from using their far greater numbers to any advantage.

I was keenly interested in seeing what the Shoshones did next. It would take a unique strategy to overcome the tactical problem they faced.

In due course I saw scores of women and children dash off to the village on a mysterious errand. They returned bearing the circular shields that belonged to their husbands and fathers.

When next the Shoshones lined up to attack, nearly every warrior had a shield on his arm. The few who didn't were placed at the rear. The front ranks, to a man, also had lances, which they held at shoulder height, cocked to thrust.

At a shout from Touch the Clouds, who once again was in personal command, they advanced in tight formation into the horseshoe. Watching them, I was reminded of accounts I had read in history books of ancient warfare involving the Greeks and the Romans, and how for many centuries the phalanx was the accepted standard of battle. In a moment of whimsy, I imagined that this must be what it had been like for those who witnessed Thermopylae, although in this case it was the larger force, not the smaller, relying on the bristling hedgehog.

As before, the Piegans let fly with clouds of arrows. But this time most of the shafts rained down without effect, thanks to the shields.

I wished we were closer. I dearly yearned to observe the entire conflict up close. To the utter astonishment of Corporal Fiske and my men, I sprang to my feet, ordered them to stay where they were, and then dashed to my mount.

None of the Shoshones tried to stop me. I came to a stop to one side of the bottleneck and rose in the stirrups. The opening was jammed with Shoshones and Piegans locked in the most violent combat. Their heated cries and the clash of arms filled the air.

When a cause is hopeless, when men know they are doomed, they fight with a savagery born of desperation. The Piegans had failed to break the Shoshone charge, and they knew they must either drive the Shoshones back or suffer extermination. So they fought with heightened ferocity.

What I beheld that day will live with me my whole life long.

At close quarters bows and arrows were useless. It was lance against knife, war club against tomahawk. The carnage was horrendous. No quarter was asked, none given. When a wounded man fell, if friends were near him they might pull him to temporary safety. If he were hemmed by enemies, they bashed out his brains or slit his throat. The thud of blows was like the beat of drums. Bones snapped like dry twigs.

Skulls were cleaved like melons. Mixed with the other sounds was the fleshy *thunk* of knives and the *thud* of tomahawks biting deep.

I saw a Piegan warrior slit a Shoshone from ear to ear, only to have a lance buried in his chest before he could blink. I saw a Shoshone plunge a knife into a Piegan, only to have the dying Piegan, in turn, bury his blade in the Shoshone. I saw another Piegan cleave clean through a Shoshone's forearm, then laugh as the Shoshone's blood spurted across his face and neck.

The havoc wreaked on both sides was horrendous. But when a Shoshone fell there was always another warrior to take his place, while for the Piegans each loss was crucial. By sheer attrition the Shoshones were wearing the Piegans down. Bodies littered the ground, some convulsing and twitching. Severed body parts were sprinkled here and there.

Eventually there were no more than a dozen Piegans left, backed against the rear of the bluff. They were caked with blood and gore, and many of their weapons were shattered or splintered. But they did not give up.

Bear Child was among them. He bore several wounds, including a wicked gash on his left temple, but not once had I seen him cry out in pain or show weakness.

There came a brief lull. The Shoshones nearly filled the horseshoe, and were massing for a final rush, when Touch the Clouds raised a blood-soaked arm and shouted. The other Shoshones stepped back.

I should have brought Jacob Hyde with me. For now Touch the Clouds addressed Bear Child in that peculiar sign talk Indians use, and Bear Child responded in kind. I wondered if Touch the Clouds was asking if the Piegans wanted to surrender. Or was it something else? Some personal exchange, man to man, leader to leader? Whatever it was, Bear Child smiled and stood taller, and then he and some of the surviving Piegans did the strangest thing you can imagine: They began to sing. As God is my witness, they stood there, caked with sweat and gore and blood, about to be annihilated, and sang at the tops of their lungs.

I have since learned that it is customary among certain tribes for those who know they are going to die to sing a death chant. What practical purpose this serves, I leave for others to decide. For my part, I thought it silly and unmanly, but I am not an Indian.

Not until much later did I realize that Touch the Clouds had halted the battle for just this reason. It was a gesture of respect to his adversaries, and my estimation of him rose several notches.

After a while the Piegans stopped singing. At Bear Child's urging, they stood closer together and firmed their grips on their weapons. Not one showed the slightest fear.

I have often heard the red race referred to as a race of craven cowards, but like so many of our beliefs concerning them, the accusation is without foundation. They are as brave as any white man alive, and some are braver than most.

From then on, I began to regard Indians differently.

Now came the moment when Touch the Clouds again raised an arm and once again shouted. This time it was a signal for the Shoshones to fall on their enemies with renewed vigor. The Piegans resisted with superhuman zeal, laying about them like madmen, but in the end the inevitable occurred: They were overwhelmed and slaughtered.

The last I saw of Bear Child, he was borne to the earth under a deluge of knives, war clubs, and tomahawks. He cut and slashed to the last, a true warrior to his dying breath.

Some moments in our lives have profound effects. This was one of those moments for me. Bowing my head in deep thought, I rode back to my command. In my mind I relived the clash—every blow, every shriek, every drop of spilled blood. I never wanted to forget.

Then a troubling thought struck me. The Piegans had fought a battle worthy of a Homeric epic, yet who would know? Who would recount their struggle for future generations? Who would emblazon their fight in the pages of history? No one. There were no survivors to carry word to the Piegan people, and the Shoshones had no written language that I knew of. The world would never hear of Bear Child's heroic stand.

I speculated on how often the same thing had happened in the past. How many anonymous men and women lost their lives in noble struggles of which there was no record? The total must be legion.

History is a harsh mistress. One man's legend is another man's lost tale. The great and the brave and the valiant have too often gone unrecognized and unsung, and therein lies tragedy, I think. Consider. Had there been no Herodotus to record the stirring sacrifice of Leonidas and the Three Hundred, would they today be enshrined in our annals as the heroes of heroes? A sobering thought for a military man.

"Are you all right, sir?" Corporal Fiske asked as I rode up.

"Fine," I said much too brusquely. "Have the men mount. We will return to the village, collect our packhorses, and leave while the Shoshones are busy with their wounded and their dead."

"What about breakfast, sir? The men haven't eaten yet."

"We still have some hardtack, don't we?" was my rejoinder.

Corporal Fiske and several troopers within earshot frowned. The little we had left was borderline rancid, but what was a little stomach discomfort compared to the agony and suffering I had just witnessed? Honestly, sometimes my men behaved like infants.

I hoped to slip away quietly, but in that I was frustrated by the arrival of Touch the Clouds and Drags the Rope. Both had sustained multiple minor wounds, and the giant was bleeding profusely.

"You are leaving?" the Shoshone leader said through his translator. His expression showed he was troubled.

"I am afraid we must," I replied. "I thank you for your hospitality."

"I hope we have not upset you. We had to do what we did. If we let them get away, they would tell their people that we are weak."

"No explanation is needed." I thought it ironic that he deemed me so squeamish. I was, after all, a military man, a warrior in my own right.

"Those traders who died." Touch the Clouds would not let it drop. "They tried to cause trouble between us and the Crows. Some of my people were killed. They were bad men, those whites."

"So you've said."

"You must understand. It is important."

The two of them looked at me in earnest appeal. "Trust me," I assured them. "I understand completely and I will do what is right." Or, to be more precise, I would do as my duty dictated.

"I trust you," Touch the Clouds said, and in a surprising gesture he had undoubtedly learned from the Kings, he offered his hand as a token of his friendship.

I smiled and shook, and with that we departed. There was no one else to see us off. The rest were tending the stricken. From the bluff rose loud weeping and lamentation. I imagined many Piegan women would share the grief of their Shoshone counterparts after Bear Child's war party failed to return.

I had never given as much consideration to the Indian way of life as I did the rest of that day. Like most of my kind, I tended to regard them as simple savages, little better than animals in some respects. But they were more like us than I ever conceived. Once you stripped away the veneer of customs and superstitions, we shared a bond that ran deeper than the color of our skins: We were all human beings.

By and large, though, their lives were a lot more precarious than ours. They had to constantly be on their guard against their many enemies as well as the many beasts that roamed the wilds. It spoke volumes about their character, about their perseverance in the face of adversity.

Did I believe Touch the Clouds's claim that the traders had been up to no good? To judge by the behavior of Phineas Borke and his friends, it was not inconceivable. But was that pertinent to my investigation? Did it really matter if the men who were massacred were decent and upright or scurrilous and contemptible? That was the crux of the matter, and one I pondered long and hard.

I sent Jacob Hyde on ahead to scout and blaze our trail, with instructions to bear east until we were near the valley Shakespeare McNair called his own. From there we would proceed south until we found the one I was looking for.

I became so absorbed in thought, I failed to appreciate the scenic splendor around us until late in the afternoon, when I was jarred from my reverie by a screech from close overhead. Glancing up, I was startled to behold a large red hawk gliding with outstretched wings not twenty feet above our heads. It looked right at me, and for a few moments I entertained the childish notion that it would swoop down. But no, it glided the length of the column, then banked and rapidly gained altitude. Its interest in us was explained by a large nest high in a giant dead tree on an adjoining slope. Its mate was there, feeding several young ones.

The woods were a wonderland of game of every kind: squirrels, chipmunks, rabbits, deer, even a few cow elk with young ones of their own. They had little fear of man, and stared in undisturbed innocence as we rode by. Eventually that would change. Eventually more and more settlers would venture west, and in another fifty years, perhaps more, the mountains would be as crowded as the East. Men like McNair and the Kings must not have been too happy about the prospect.

That evening we made camp on a grassy shelf. In a nook at one end was a spring, the water so clear we could see every pebble on the bottom. Hyde and Clemens went off to forage for our supper and brought back a fine black-tailed buck. It had to weigh three hundred pounds. I thought it remarkable, but our scout said it was middling size. At that time of year, the really big ones were higher up. Some, he claimed, would top the scales at close to five hundred pounds. I found that difficult to swallow. White-tailed bucks seldom exceeded three hundred. But then, I had to remember that west of the Mississippi, the animals were generally bigger, the rivers undeniably swifter, and the mountains ten times higher.

I was dallying over a cup of coffee when Corporal Fiske sank down beside me and said, "Mind if I ask you a question, sir?"

"By all means." I still did not think all that highly of him, but his company had become more bearable since Sergeant Wheatridge's death.

"Some of the men and I have been wondering, sir, how much longer it will be before we return to Fort Leavenworth."

"Miss your creature comforts, do you, Corporal?"

"There's that, sir, yes. But it's mainly we've been away for months now, and some of the men have wives and kids. Those of us who don't—well, we just plain miss being among our own kind."

I harbored similar sentiments and found the best thing to do was suppress them.

"Lord knows, the life of a soldier isn't anything to crow about, sir. But some parts are better than others, and this"—Fiske motioned to encompass our surroundings,—"this wears on a man after a while."

"That it does, Corporal," I agreed. "But so long as we wear the uniforms of the United States Army, we have a responsibility to our country to carry out our orders to the best of our ability. You can tell the men we'll head back when we have done what we were sent out to do, and not before."

"Yes, sir." Corporal Fiske made no attempt to hide his disappointment.

"Duty is a two-edged sword," I mentioned. "We can't lose sight of our reason for being here. If we do, there's a danger of letting our personal feelings over-shadow our professional commitment."

"There you go again with those big words, sir." Corporal Fiske grinned. "I'll just tell the men you can't say yet how much longer it will be. They'll have to be patient." He appraised me a moment. "It's Zach King, isn't it? We're on our way to his place to question him about the massacre?"

"It's long overdue. He's the key to this whole affair."

"What if he won't cooperate, sir? Or if he flat-out denies having anything to do with it?"

"My orders were to do whatever is necessary to get to the bottom of this. If I have to, I'll drag Zach King clear back to the post. And if he resists, then so much the worse for him."

# Chapter Twelve

The valley was wider than McNair's but not as long. It, too, was favored by a stream that flowed out of the northwest, made a large S, then meandered off to the southeast. The cabin was situated along the west edge of the valley, within rifle range of a wooded slope, which I thought careless. The corral was separate, another mistake, since hostiles could easily steal the stock. Several small outbuildings completed the homestead.

As we descended, I insisted Jacob Hyde stay with the detachment. I made no secret of our approach. I wanted him to know we were coming. His reaction would prove instructive.

No sooner had we started across the valley floor than Hyde pointed at a line of fresh hoofprints. They came from the north and led straight to the cabin. "See there? Someone was riding hard. Yesterday morning or so."

I could guess who it was. We had forty yards to go when a curtain moved. I glimpsed a face, then the door opened a couple of inches and the muzzle of a rifle appeared.

"That's far enough!"

I brought the column to a halt. The owner of the rifle had a voice much too high to be a man. "Mrs. Zachary King? I'm Lieutenant Pickforth. Sorry to disturb you, but we're here on official business."

The door opened and she stepped onto the porch, a Hawken wedged to her shoulder. She was younger than I expected. I also expected her to be Shoshone or a half-blood, like her husband, but she was white through and through. Lustrous sandy hair framed her small ears, and she had the most fetching blue eyes. Buckskins sculpted her slender figure. They lent her a mannish aspect that in no way diminished her appeal. She was not what I would call a raving beauty, but neither was she a plain Jane. Her face, in particular, appealed to me greatly.

"State your business and be off."

I had to smile at her presumption. "Would that it were possible. But I'm afraid I must speak with you *and* your husband." I glanced at the corral, where a single horse dozed in the sun. "Is he home, by any chance?"

"No, he's not. He went off into the high country on an elk hunt several days ago and won't be back for two or three weeks."

Jacob Hyde leaned toward me to whisper, "That's a damned lie. This time of year there are plenty of elk hereabouts. You saw some yourself, remember? No need for anyone to go up after them."

To Mrs. King I said, "I am sorry to hear that. Perhaps you would be so kind as to let me talk with you, then?"

She had a delightful habit of chewing her lower lip when making a decision. "I suppose it can't hurt. But just you. No one else. The rest can camp yonder." She pointed across the valley at where the stream flowed in a wide loop.

"You heard the lady," I told Corporal Fiske. "It shouldn't take more than an hour, I should think."

Phineas Borke nudged his horse closer to mine. "Take me with you. It's my brother her husband killed. I have a right to question the bitch, don't I?"

"No. And you will kindly refrain from insulting her." I cannot tell you how sorry I was that the colonel made me bring Borke and his friends along. "In case you've forgotten, under our legal system a person is presumed innocent until they're proven guilty, not the other way around."

"What more proof do you need?" This from Jacob Hyde. "I told you I saw Zach King plain as day."

"You also said the Shoshones were involved, but so far all the evidence, and all the witnesses, point to the Crows." I lifted my reins. "No, gentlemen. You will go with my men to the stream."

I could feel their eyes bore into my back as I rode to a hitch rail and climbed down. Their eyes were not the only ones. Zach King's wife watched me with the same wary intensity as the red hawk had earlier. I removed my gauntlets, slapped dust from my uniform,

and climbed the steps. "I am pleased to make your acquaintance, Mrs. King."

"Call me Lou." She offered her hand. "It's short for Louisa. My maiden name was Clark."

I turned toward the door, thinking she would invite me in, but she indicated a rocking chair. "Have a seat. Would you care for refreshment? Tea, perhaps? Or coffee? I have a jug of apple cider, too. We bought a bushel of apples from some emigrants with a wagon train not long ago."

"That sounds delightful. You are most gracious."

She glanced at the column, which had moved off, then went inside. I heard her rummaging around, and after a while she reappeared. The cider was delicious. I savored each sip while studying her over the glass.

"So what is so important, Lieutenant?" she goaded when I did not bring it up quickly enough to suit her.

"I believe you already know. I believe your neighbor, Shakespeare McNair, paid you a visit yesterday and told you why we are here. And that he and your husband are off somewhere waiting for my men and me to leave."

My frankness caught her by surprise. She tried not to let her emotions show, but she lacked the guile of a sophisticate or a wanton. "Your being here can come to no good. Go away and leave us be."

"I can't do that, Mrs. King. Not until certain questions are answered to my satisfaction." I did not bandy words. "For instance, did your husband have a hand in the massacre of the men at the trading post? If so, he has to answer for his deeds."

"What happened, happened. It's not worth all this fuss."

"We are talking about the loss of human lives." I tried to be stern with her, but she was so appealing, I could not bring myself to treat her with anything other than the utmost courtesy.

"Some loss is worse than others" was her response. "If a sheriff shot a killer who was about to kill someone else, would you call that wrong?"

"Your analogy leaves something to be desired. The men who were slain were traders, not killers."

"That's where you're wrong, Lieutenant. Artemis Borke incited the Crows to kill Shoshones. He even gave them new rifles so they could do the job right. It's the same as if he pulled the triggers himself."

"You have proof of this allegation?"

"We know the Crows got the rifles from him. What more proof do you need?"

"Considerably more." I sipped some cider. "Arrange an interview with your husband for me. I promise to come alone and unarmed, if he desires. Make sure he understands my men and I are not leaving until I've spoken to him."

Louisa was gnawing on her lip again. "I told you. He's up in the high country."

"Do you take me for a simpleton, madam? No man in his right mind would ride off and leave an attractive woman such as yourself to the tender mercies of a platoon of soldiers."

She gave a start and touched a hand to her hair. "Do you really think I'm attractive?"

If I live to be a hundred, I will never understand women. You have probably heard every man you know say the same, but it's not our fault. Women are the most mystifying creatures on God's green earth. Their minds take convoluted twists and leaps of logic that defy rational thought. For instance, here was Louisa King, a married woman dearly concerned for the welfare of a husband accused of the most perfidious of crimes, and when I made an offhand remark about her charms, she focused on that and not the issue at hand. Now I ask you, is that logical?

"Let's not stray too far afield, Mrs. King. How soon can you set up a meeting with Zach?"

I swear, at the rate she was going, she wouldn't have a lower lip left before the day was done. Her eyes flicked to a mountain to the south, and she wrung her slender hands around the Hawken. "How about first thing tomorrow morning? I can't sneak off to see him until nightfall."

"Why wait that long? Why not go now?"

She looked across the valley at the camp my men were setting up. "I hear tell Artemis Borke's brother is with you. He and some friends."

"Phineas Borke, yes. He's responsible for us being here."

Louisa leaned her rifle against a post. "I also hear you have a scout by the name of Jacob Hyde."

"Also true. He witnessed the atrocity."

"Did he indeed?" Her thin eyebrows arched. "Did he tell you about him and my father-in-law, Nate King? About the bad blood between them?"

"He did not."

"I have the story from Nate's own mouth. It was some time ago, fifteen years or so. They were trappers at the time. Hyde had himself a Nez Percé wife. At the rendezvous, he got drunk and something she said sent him into a rage. He beat her, right out there in front of everybody, beat her awful, and he'd have gone on beating her except that my father-in-law took the branch he was using away from him. That made Hyde even madder, and he pulled a knife, but Nate picked Hyde up over his head and threw him against a tree, and that was that. Jacob Hyde has hated my father-in-law ever since."

I believed her. There wasn't a duplicitous bone in her body. "So you're saying Jacob Hyde never actually saw your husband at the trading post? That he made it up to get back at your husband's father for something that happened all those years ago?" Hyde had already admitted that he wasn't fond of Nate King, but I couldn't quite conceive of anyone harboring so much hatred for so long.

"All I'm saying is that I don't trust Borke or Hyde as far as I can fling this cabin. They have it in for the Kings and will stop at nothing to get even."

Contemplating her allegation, I drank the rest of my cider. She misconstrued my silence. It made her nervous, and after fidgeting and shifting her weight from one foot to the other, she couldn't take it anymore.

"Listen, I don't expect you to take my word for it. But as God is my witness, I'm telling the truth. Ask Shakespeare McNair about the incident at the rendezvous. He was there."

"I daresay McNair is a tad biased. In my presence he referred to Nate King as, and I quote, 'the son he never had.'" I handed her the glass. "Can you think of anyone else who can corroborate your story?"

Sadly shaking her head, Louisa said, "Most of the trappers who were there gave up the trade after the beaver market crashed. Of the few who stuck, all except a handful have gone to their reward."

"That's too bad." I rose and moved to the rail. "Shall we say tomorrow morning, about an hour after sunup?"

"You'll come alone and unarmed? Just like you promised?"

"I am a man of my word." I put a finger to my hat brim.

As I slowly rode toward camp, I was at war with myself. My head and my heart were at odds. I knew the truth, you see. I knew beyond any shadow of doubt that Zachary King had indeed had a hand in the massacre. The full extent had yet to be determined, but that was only a matter of time.

A reception committee was waiting: Phineas Borke, Clemens, Sewell, and Jacob Hyde.

"Well?" the former demanded as I reined in.

"Well what?" His tone rankled.

"What did the breed-lover have to say?"

"I warned you before about watching your mouth." As I slid down, Corporal Fiske and several privates hurried to my side. "As for our discussion, it's none of your business, Mr. Borke."

"Like hell!" Phineas exploded. "It was my brother her rotten husband killed! I'd say that gives me more of a stake in the outcome than anyone else."

"That it does," Clemens backed him, and wagged a finger at me. "It's about damn time you did your job."

I fought down my anger and calmly answered, "What makes you gentlemen think I'm not?"

Jacob Hyde answered. "It's as plain as the nose on my face. If you believed my version of the massacre, you wouldn't keep askin' everyone we meet about who's to blame. You've been dead set against us from the beginnin'."

"That's absurd." I would never let personal feelings influence the performance of my duty.

"Is it?" Phineas Borke poked me in the chest. "I say you're a damned liar."

My fist connected with his chin before I realized I had swung. I hit him so hard that he crashed to the ground, flat on his back. I think everyone was shocked, myself most of all. Clemens and Sewell came toward me, but for once Corporal Fiske showed some initiative and he and the troopers planted themselves in front of me.

"Don't even think it," the corporal declared.

"Lay a hand on our lieutenant and you answer to us," Private Bittles said.

A prickly sensation spread from my neck to the top of my head. I didn't quite know what to say. Their display of loyalty was as unexpected as it was touching. Until this moment, I'd assumed they regarded me in the same unflattering light I regarded them. It was a revelation of the first order.

Phineas Borke did not share my warm feelings. Rubbing his chin, he stiffly rose. "I knew it," he growled. "I knew the army couldn't be counted on to do what needs doing."

"How is that again?" I found my voice.

"You heard me. I've suspected all along that the reason your colonel picked a kid like you was so we'd go back empty-handed."

"You're being more preposterous by the minute."

"Am I? Zach King should be taken into custody and hauled to Fort Leavenworth to stand trial. But the army doesn't want to rile his friends, the Shoshones. So Templeton sends the most incompetent officer he has."

I regret not appreciating the full depth of his spite. Rather glibly, I responded, "Permit me to be the first to congratulate you on your extraordinary imagination."

"Go to hell," Borke spat. He gestured at his friends, and they walked toward the stream. Over his shoulder he fired a last verbal volley. "You'd have been smart to do what's right instead of playin' favorites. My brother wasn't a saint, but he was the only brother I had, and I'll be damned if I'll let his stinkin' murderers go on breathin'."

"Taking the law into your own hands won't solve anything," I said.

"Care to bet?"

# Chapter Thirteen

The news was imparted to me the next morning by Corporal Fiske, who burst into my tent as I was shaving. "Sir! Borke and his two friends are gone! They stole away in the middle of the night."

I paused with my straight razor to my throat. Without Borke to prosecute a formal complaint, the charge against Zach King would be dropped. It meant we could leave for Fort Leavenworth anytime I wanted.

Corporal Fiske wasn't done. "Jacob Hyde is gone, too."

A scout is essential to a wilderness campaign. Without one, finding water and food becomes a challenge that can end up costing lives. "Regrettable" was all I said, so as not to have the men worry.

"Strange, though," Corporal Fiske commented offhandedly.

"What is, Corporal?" I scraped a few final hairs from my chin.

"I'm not much of a tracker, but even I can tell they went west instead of east. Why would they do that if they were bound for home?"

"West?" Worry speared through me like a Shoshone lance. "Have my horse saddled. I want six troopers ready to accompany me in ten minutes."

"Where to, sir?"

"The King cabin."

"Why would they go there? Mrs. King isn't about to help them find her husband."

"Not deliberately, no."

I kept telling myself I was wrong. That surely Borke wouldn't do anything drastic. Then I remembered our heated exchange and the raw hatred that blazed in his beady eyes. I should have foreseen this. I should have placed Borke and his companions under guard. Someone once told me that negligence is the bane of an officer's existence, and truer words were never uttered.

The sun was only half an hour high, but I trusted that Louisa would forgive me for being early should my anxiety prove groundless. I crossed the valley floor at a gallop and vaulted from my saddle. My boot was on the bottom step when I saw that the door was ajar, and just inside was an overturned chair.

"Mrs. King?"

I barged in without knocking. A table had been knocked over and personal belongings were scattered about, a testament to the struggle she put up. A bright smear of blood by the bedroom doorway compounded my fear. The blood hadn't dried yet, so they couldn't have taken her that long ago.

"Did you see this over here, sir?" one of my men asked.

Jammed onto a peg by the front door was a crumpled sheet of paper. On it was a scrawled note:

*Breed,*
  *We have your woman. If you want to see her alive,
come alone to Lizard Rock by sunset.*

That was all. No mention of where Lizard Rock
was to be found. I reasoned it must be a well-known
landmark, at least to men familiar with the region like
Jacob Hyde and Zach King. Turning to the trooper
who had noticed the note, I instructed him, "Tell
Corporal Fiske to break camp. I want everyone here
within half an hour or there will be hell to pay."

"Yes, sir." He saluted, did an about-face, and flew
off.

I went out and sat on the porch. Louisa's abduction
presented a host of problems. For starters, Borke insisted that Zach King go alone. If I and my men
showed up, Borke might harm Louisa to spite us.
Odds were, he planned to harm her anyway, but I
would deal with that when the time came.

Another problem was her husband's absence. King
was lying low until we were gone. He had no inkling
of his wife's predicament, and unless word reached
him without delay, he might not arrive at Lizard Rock
in time.

I suppose a case could be made that this was beyond
my legal purview. The Army does not meddle in ci-
vilian affairs. Neither is the Army an arm of the law
in the sense of a marshal or a sheriff. But I was the
one who indirectly brought this down on Louisa
King's head, and I would not be able to live with myself if my lapse in judgment cost the woman her life.

Then there was the matter of what do with Borke
and his friends once I caught up to them. Ideally, I
was required to take them back to the fort and turn

them over to the proper civil authorities. Which meant Borke's charge against Lou's husband would stand—and put this whole mess right back where it started.

I considered the situation from every angle and had not yet arrived at a settled decision when Corporal Fiske and the rest of the detachment arrived. I filled him in as we rode south.

"So where are we off to now, sir, if I may be so bold?"

I pointed at the mountain Louisa King had glanced at during my talk with her. That was where I believed I would find her spouse. The top was barren; from it, a person had an unobstructed view of the entire valley.

Since several search parties can cover ground much more quickly then one, I divided my men into three groups. I led one, Fiske another, Bittles the third, but only after I informed them that, whereas I had lost my sergeant, and whereas I needed at least two subordinates of rank, and whereas we were in the grip of a crisis, I was exercising my right to make field promotions and promoted Corporal Fiske to sergeant and Private Bittles to corporal. I would attend to the necessary paperwork once we were back at the fort.

Needless to say, Fiske and Bittles were elated.

I was stretching regulations a tad. Ordinarily, the Army permits field promotions only under battlefield conditions. But there are exceptions, and I was confident I could convince Colonel Templeton it was necessary.

I ordered Sergeant Fiske to take the west slope, Corporal Bittles to take the east. I went straight up. That left the south slope as a potential avenue of escape. To foil such an attempt, I commanded four troopers to ride like hell to the south side of the mountain and keep their eyes peeled for Zach King and McNair.

I'm no fool. I knew the mountain men might easily evade us. That's why I also instructed Fiske and Bittles to do as I was doing: Every ten yards or so I cupped a hand to my mouth and shouted, "Zach King! Your wife is in grave danger! We need to talk!"

For over an hour we climbed, avoiding deadfalls and talus, and I had about worn my throat raw when we came within sight of the bald summit. Again I raised a hand to my lips. Again I called out. I don't know what kind of response I was expecting, but it certainly wasn't the crack of a rifle and the *thwack* of a slug striking a tree not two feet to my left.

"That's as close as you come!"

I brought my men to a stop. "Zachary King? I'm Lieutenant Pickforth, Second Cavalry, Detachment A, out of Fort Leavenworth."

"I know who you are. What was that you said about my wife?"

He was above us, close to the tree line, I suspected, but if so, he hid himself extraordinarily well. "She has been abducted, Mr. King, and her life is in dire jeopardy."

"How do I know this isn't a trick?"

"You have my solemn word as an officer." When he didn't reply, I thought to add, "Shakespeare McNair has met me. Ask him whether he believes I can be trusted or not."

"McNair isn't here."

I was skeptical. With my own eyes I had seen the tracks of a shod horse entering the valley from the north; there had been no recent tracks going in the other direction. "If that's the case, then all I can say is that I want to do whatever I can to help free your wife from Phineas Borke's clutches before she comes to harm."

Where he came from, I can't exactly say. One instant he wasn't there, the next he was. And nowhere near where I surmised. Not only that, he was mounted on a pinto and cradling a Hawken. He rode boldly toward us, his gaze locked on me.

Envision, if you will, a strikingly handsome stripling clad in intricately beaded buckskins and moccasins. Of wiry, muscular build, he was uncommonly broad at the shoulders and would stand close to six feet in his bare feet. Like most frontiersmen he was a living arsenal; besides the Hawken, he had a pair of flintlocks, a Green River knife, and a tomahawk tucked under his wide leather belt. The usual ammo pouch, powder horn, and leather pouch were slung across his chest.

As he came nearer, I saw that his black hair was worn loose, not braided, as many Indians liked. He had the high cheekbones typical of a Shoshone, and there was the stamp of his mother's lineage in the cast of his profile, but his eyes were vivid green, a legacy of his father's inheritance, and his English was as flawless as mine, if tinged with latent resentment.

"So you're the high-and-mighty white who has come to arrest me."

His contempt angered me even more than his unjustified racial slur. "I take it you don't think highly of white men, Mr. King."

"They've never given me reason to."

"Yet you married a white woman. You're either a hypocrite or you're deluding yourself." I was secretly tickled at the crimson tinge that flushed his face.

"I am Stalking Coyote of the Shoshone, and I answer to no man, white or red." He defiantly jutted his chin toward me, and I was reminded of a petulant child. This was the holy terror who slaughtered the traders? "Everyone answers to someone" was my retort. "None of us are as free as we would like to be."

"Speak for yourself, white man."

For the life of me, I couldn't imagine what Louisa saw in him. "We can sit here bandying insults all day, or we can save your wife. Which will it be?"

"The brother of Artemis Borke has taken her?"

I nodded and produced the note. "He left this." As King read it, I went on. "Three others are with him. One is a mountain man you might know, Jacob Hyde."

"They are dead men," Zach said. Crumpling the note, he threw it to the ground. "I will gut them and shove their intestines down their throats until they choke."

"You wouldn't," I said. But I could tell by his expression that, yes, he surely would, and possibly do far worse before he was done. Suddenly I saw this man-child half-breed in a whole new light.

"They have brought it on their own heads."

"It must be convenient being your own judge, jury, and executioner," I commented. "But that's not how whites do things."

"You left the white world when you crossed the Mississippi, Lieutenant Pickforth. The wilderness is a world all its own. Here, we survive by our wits and our strength and our readiness to kill when we need to. Here, our freedom is absolute. And with that freedom comes absolute responsibility for our actions."

I confess to being amazed. Just a minute earlier he had acted like an indignant child; now here he was uttering as profound a statement as I ever heard. He was an enigma, this Zachary King. I noticed, too, that he had done me the courtesy of addressing me by my rank and name. "I want you to know I blame myself for your wife's abduction. I was remiss in not keeping an eye on Borke and his friends."

"The blame is mine," King said. "I should not have listened to my wife and Uncle Shakespeare and come up here to wait for you to leave. My place was by my wife's side."

"Where is McNair, anyhow?" I inquired.

"He went to fetch my father."

So the legendary Nate King would soon arrive. "What good did McNair think that would do?"

A smile quirked Zach's lips. "Have you ever been caught in a flood or an avalanche?"

I failed to see what that had to do with anything. "I can't say as I have, no. How is that pertinent?"

"They have a lot in common with my father. He is not like most men, Lieutenant. I cannot expect you to understand, but he believes highly in absolute freedom, and when he is crossed, the result is the same as being swept away by a flood or tons of snow."

"You're saying he would gut Borke and the others, too?"

"No, Lieutenant. My father always kills cleanly. I have more of my mother in me. I only kill cleanly when those I kill deserve it. Borke and his companions do not. For what they have done, they must suffer before they die."

"I'm sorry. I can't allow that."

"What you want is irrelevant."

He was sorely trying my patience. "Listen closely, Mr. King. I have a duty to my country to uphold its laws to the fullest extent of which I am capable. Even here in the wilderness. I can't allow you to indulge your lust for spilling blood."

He laughed.

"You find that amusing?"

"I am always amused by those who think everyone else should think as they do. The world is not part of you, Lieutenant, you are part of the world."

There he was again, being profound. "You can call it what you want. The fact remains, we are going after your wife together, and I will not permit you to harm Borke or anyone else once we have caught up to them. Is that understood?"

Again he laughed.

God, he was infuriating. I had never met anyone who baffled me so. "I want your word that you will do as I say, Mr. King. If you refuse, I'll have you relieved of your weapons, bound, and gagged."

"Try to bind me, Lieutenant, and you will lose two or three of your men, if not more." King grinned. "But if it will soothe your ruffled feathers, I promise not to try and rub out Borke and the others so long as I am with you."

His grin fueled my anger. Here I was, doing my best to keep him from making a mistake he would long regret, and he was treating me like I was a simpleton. "Very well." To Private Howard I said, "Fire three shots into the air." That was the signal for Sergeant Fiske, Corporal Bittles, and the men I had sent south to rejoin us.

"May I ask you a question, Lieutenant?" Zach King inquired.

His politeness made me suspicious. "So long as it isn't too personal."

"Are all army officers like you?"

"More or less. Why do you ask?"

"Oh, no reason." And he laughed a third time.

# Chapter Fourteen

Lizard Rock was not, as I supposed, high up in the mountains. It was out on the prairie, a boulder sixty feet high sculpted by the elements into some semblance of the reptile it was named after. Or so Zachary King informed me as we wound steadily lower through the foothills.

He and I were at the head of the column, Sergeant Fiske and Corporal Bittles next in line behind us, Bittles unable to stop beaming with joy at his promotion. After hours of hard travel I still did not quite know what to make of King.

He was a consummate tracker, I'll say that for him. Bent low over the pinto, he had stuck like glue to Borke's trail from the point where it left the cabin. "They've stayed in single file," he related. "My wife's horse is behind Borke's. Hyde came last and stopped often to check their back trail."

"You can't be sure it's Hyde," I said to nettle him.

"He wears moccasins. The rest wear boots." King pointed at trampled grass and a patch of earth. "There is where he climbed down to relieve himself. You can see his footprints as plain as day."

He could, maybe. All I saw were scuff marks. "Where did you learn to track so expertly?"

"I had the best teachers alive. My father, Uncle Shakespeare, Touch the Clouds, and others. By the time I was ten, I was better than men twice my age."

Humility was not his strong suit. "Why do you keep calling McNair your 'uncle'? To my knowledge, the two of you aren't related."

118

"Not by blood, no. But he's been part of our family since before I was born. I've called him uncle for as long as I can remember."

"He must think highly of you to have nearly ridden his horse into the ground to warn you."

Zach glanced at me. "Do you throw your line out after real fish now and then, too?"

"No use denying it. You've already admitted McNair came to see you. In the civilized world, the law would call that obstruction of justice."

"The law doesn't mean much out here."

"It should. Men can't live without laws and rules. It's how we keep the lid on our darkest yearnings, and mold order out of chaos. Without laws we're no better than animals."

"My mother always says that wanting to do good must come from inside us, not from being told to. She got that from her parents. Shoshones don't believe in punishing their children like whites do."

"Why do I have the feeling you're partial to her side of your family tree?" I was being more than a little sarcastic.

"If you always had whites looking down their noses at you over an accident of birth, you wouldn't think so highly of them, either." Zach's features clouded. "Ever since I can remember, I'm been treated like scum for no other reason than I'm half-and-half."

He had me there. Prejudice against half-bloods was epidemic, even back east. Or should I say more so back there? In the rarefied social circles in which I'd traveled before storming out on my father to enlist, the prejudice was sweeping. Blacks, Indians, Orientals—anyone who wasn't white was viewed as inferior.

"Now some whites have gone and kidnapped my wife, and you wonder why I'm partial to my mother's side of the family?" King scoffed.

"They did it out of revenge, not because they're bigots," I reminded him. "And you can't hardly blame Phineas Borke for being mad at you for killing his brother and the men with him."

"I didn't kill all of—" Zach began, then caught himself and glared. "Clever. Real clever. But it's not like I had a lot of choice. Artemis had to be stopped or he'd have sparked a war between the Shoshones and the Crows. He was a killer posing as a respectable trader to hoodwink the Indians."

"Do you realize what you've just done?"

"So what?" He sighed. "Do you know why Shakespeare and Lou wanted me gone when you got there? Because I never lie. Ever. My folks never did, and they raised me to be the same. So yes, Lieutenant, I killed Artemis Borke, and if I had it to do over again, I'd kill him again. And good riddance."

"There are times, Mr. King, when silence is wiser than the truth."

"I've never claimed to be all that smart." Damn me if he didn't grin. "But I've always spoken with a straight tongue. How many can say the same?"

"You mystify me, Mr. King. I can't make up my mind if you're one of the most honest individuals I've ever met or one of the biggest fools."

We were nearing the last of the foothills. Beyond stretched the prairie. Zach King glanced at me several times as we climbed the final slope, and when we reached the crown he drew rein and announced, "This is as far as you and your men go."

I raised my arm to bring the column to a halt. "That isn't for you to decide."

"Like hell it's not. You read the note. I'm to come alone. If I don't, they'll harm Lou." He pointed his

Hawken at my chest. "So whether you like it or not, you're staying here."

"You'll be riding right into their gun sights."

"Do you think I don't know that? It's why they picked Lizard Rock. They can post a lookout on top and spot anyone coming from miles off. All the more reason for me to go it by my lonesome."

I noticed Sergeant Fiske inching a hand toward the hammer of his rifle and shook my head. To King I said, "Your only hope is to show up there just as the sun is going down."

"I know." He surprised me by kneeing his paint close enough to reach out a hand and shake mine. "It was interesting making your acquaintance, Lieutenant. It was too bad you had to come all this way for nothing."

"It isn't over yet," I assured him, but he wasn't listening. He had started down the hill, shifting so he covered me until he was convinced we wouldn't try to stop him. Then he goaded the paint to a trot and was soon raising dust out on the plain.

"We're letting him go, sir?" Sergeant Fiske asked.

"You should know me better than that by now." I watched until the dust was barely visible, then I gigged my mount and shouted, "Forward, ho!"

Fiske brought his animal up alongside mine. "What about the woman, sir?" He had to raise his voice to be heard above the drum of hooves. "If those polecats spot us, won't they figure King is to blame and kill her?"

"They're not going to spot us," I declared. "Don't worry. I have it all worked out." To tell the truth, I was quite pleased with myself. Here was a golden opportunity to wrap everything up in one fell swoop. Afterward, well, I would take it one step at a time.

## David Thompson

I recalled King saying that Lizard Rock was six miles out. Allowing for the amount of daylight left, I figured he would go only a mile or two before he stopped to wait for sunset. Consequently, I went only half a mile, then I reined to the north. In order to ensure that King didn't spot us, I rode about four miles before I reined east again. This put us parallel with him. When we had gone another mile, I called a halt. Ordering the men to climb down, I bid them gather in front of me.

"Most of you are probably wondering what we are up to. It's simple. We are going to assist Zachary King in rescuing his wife whether he wants us to or not. To that end, we must outwit both him and those who abducted her." I elaborated on my ploy, which met with smiles and nods of assent.

"I concede there's a risk," I concluded my speech. "But it can't be helped. I'll take full responsibility. I, and I alone, will be punished should anything go wrong."

There was nothing to do then but mark the passage of the sun.

My stomach spawned a swarm of butterflies. It was noble of me to talk about accepting the blame if anything went amiss, but it was Louisa King, not I, who would pay the supreme price. The thought of bearing the burden of her death for the rest of my days sent a shudder down my spine. I liked her. I liked her a lot. I could never forgive myself if things went wrong.

The moment came. The sun was balanced on the rim of the world, a great blazing orange ball about to bid its domain adieu. I ordered the men to mount and we galloped east until we were six miles from the foothills, or as close to it as my educated guess allowed. Here I drew rein and left the horses in the keeping of

122

four troopers. The rest accompanied me at the double to the south.

My plan was to come up on Lizard Rock from the north at about the same time Zach King approached it from the west. The eyes of Borke and his friends would be on King, so in theory, my men and I should be able to sneak up quite close without being seen. Once Louisa was safe, I would deal with her abductors.

Then there was the other business to conclude.

Before starting out, I took the precaution of having my men remove every item on their person that might rattle or clink or make noise of any kind. Except for the scuff of our boots, we ran in silence until I spied what at first glance seemed to be a small hill. I immediately signaled to go to ground, and from that point on, we crawled.

The sun was on the verge of relinquishing its rule of the firmament to blossoming stars, and twilight had plunged the prairie into gray gloom. My elbows and knees were scuffed and sore, and I had a crick in my neck from constantly craning it. By my reckoning we had a hundred yards to cover when a shot rang out and shouting ensued.

I came to a stop and carefully rose onto one knee. Lizard Rock, in silhouette, did not resemble a lizard so much as it resembled a cow, I thought, which was neither here nor there.

At its base figures moved, and they interested me more. As did the lone rider astride a paint, approaching from the west. Zach King was reloading. Evidently he had fired a shot to apprise them of his arrival.

Phineas Borke had one hand looped around Louisa King's neck. The other held a pistol pressed to her head. Clemens and Sewell had rifles trained on her husband.

I peered so intently that my eyes started to hurt, but I did not see Jacob Hyde, and that worried me. He might be on the other side of Lizard Rock, in which case we had nothing to fear. But what if he was on top of the rock? There must be a way up. Zach King had mentioned that it made an excellent lookout.

I flattened and resumed crawling. We had come this far. I could not change my mind now.

Zach King drew rein and said barely loud enough for me to hear, "I've done as you wanted, Borke. Let my wife go, you son of a bitch."

"I was beginnin' to think you valued your hide more than hers," Phineas Borke responded. "Another couple of minutes and I'd have splattered her brains all over the grass."

Lou tried to wrest free, but he was too strong for her. To Zach she declared, "You shouldn't have! I don't care what happens to me so long as you're all right."

Clemens had a brittle laugh. "I swear. Keep this up, you two, and I'm liable to break into tears."

Zach was studying Lizard Rock. "Where's Jacob Hyde?"

"Don't you fret none about him," Borke said. "He's where he can do the most good if you don't do exactly as we tell you."

King didn't like that, and neither did I. Again I scoured the landmark from top to bottom, but the scout was too well concealed. I crawled more slowly than before, for now there was a very real chance the blackguards might hear us.

"Let my wife go," Zach King repeated.

"Not until you've shed that Hawken and your belly guns," Borke told him. "And your knife and tomahawk, now that I think of it."

"Don't!" Louisa cried. "You'll be at their mercy!"

Angrily shaking her, Borke rasped, "That's the general idea, woman! I aim to have me some fun with your breed before I do him in. I want to hear him cry and beg and grovel at my feet."

"That will never happen," Zach King said.

"Think so?" Borke sneered. "Hell, boy. You ever been tortured? I'll do things to you that will curl your toes—if you have any when I get done."

Lou's face was pale in the gathering gloom. "I'd rather die than have my husband suffer. Do with me as you will. But Zach, don't you dare drop your guns."

Borke hissed and pressed his pistol against her temple. "What will it be, half-breed? How much do you care for this piece of trash? Do I squeeze the trigger? Or do I let her live?"

"I have no guarantee you'll honor your word and let her go," Zach rightly noted. "Until she's safe, it would be stupid of me to disarm."

"You'll do it, by God," Borke fumed, "or I'll kill her right this instant! So help me I will!"

Zach leveled his Hawken. "And I will kill you a second after you do."

It was almost too dark for me to make them out. Or, for that matter, for my men to see them, and they needed to be able to when I gave the signal to open fire. I had to make my move soon. But I was waiting for Borke to lower his pistol.

Sewell cursed luridly. "This is gettin' us nowhere, Phineas. Let's kill the bitch and this stinkin' half-blood and be done with it."

I sighted down my rifle at Borke and to my dismay discovered I could not fix a definite bead. I might hit Louisa by mistake.

Phineas Borke was a lot of things, few of them flattering, but one thing he was not was stupid. "Let's not be hasty, boys." He was taking Zach's threat seriously and would not risk taking a slug. "I'm sure the breed will come to his senses if he has a minute to think about it."

A tense silence fell. I started to rise, thinking that maybe I could get a better shot. Some of the troopers nearest me took that as their cue to do the same, and when they did, so did those behind us, with the unintended result that nearly my entire command stood up at the same moment. Even as dark as it was, I feared we would not go unnoticed, and my fear was justified, for hardly had I straightened when a harsh shout arose atop Lizard Rock, courtesy of Jacob Hyde.

"Look out, Phineas! It's the soldiers!"

At that, Hyde's rifle boomed, and without being commanded to, some of my men replied, and then everyone was firing at once. Instead of effecting Louisa King's rescue, my carefully executed plan had placed her in dire peril.

# Chapter Fifteen

Those were terrible moments. Lead was flying every which way, and I could not be sure of who was who. I held my fire and bellowed for my men to desist, but few heard me above the roar of rifles and pistols and the cries of one of my troopers, who was bawling, "I've been hit! I've been hit!"

Horses whinnied, and then hooves drummed, and the shooting slackened enough for me to make myself heard. "Cease firing!"

I barreled toward the spot where I had last seen Louisa King, and she was there, all right, but on the ground, her head cradled in Zach King's lap. Half her face was a black smear, but the color was deceptive. In the light of day it would be scarlet.

King looked at me, his anguish a mirror of my own. "They killed her! The bastards killed her!" Suddenly easing her to the ground, he took a couple of bounds and vaulted onto his paint. Wheeling it, he raced in pursuit.

"Wait!" I shouted, but I might as well have whispered it, because he was too racked by grief to listen.

Sergeant Fiske materialized at my side. "Privates Walker and Aberdeen have been wounded, sir."

"How badly?" I mechanically asked. I could not tear my gaze off the still form at my feet.

"I need to get a fire going to tell for sure."

"Then do so. And send a detail to have the horses brought up right away. We are not letting those murderers escape." I knelt beside Louisa. In death she looked so frail, like a fragile flower stricken in the prime of its beauty. I touched her cheek and my fingertips were damp with blood. Bending down, I sought the bullet wound but could not find one. I assumed it must be covered by her hair, but when I gingerly probed for a bullet hole, all I found was a gash on the right side, just above her ear. The bullet had grazed her. Puzzled, and tingling with hope, I felt her neck for a pulse and there it was, faint but undeniable. "She's alive!" I exclaimed.

## David Thompson

In his grief and thirst for vengeance, Zach King had rushed off too soon.

I bid Corporal Bittles and several others carry Louisa over to the fire Sergeant Fiske was stoking on the south side of Lizard Rock, where it was out of the wind. I ordered blankets brought and had her bundled in them, then directed that a pot of water be rapidly brought to a boil and one of the blankets be cut into strips to use as bandages. The men fell over themselves in their eagerness to help.

Say what you will about the males of our kind, say that they are crude and uncouth and solely interested in carnal pleasures, say that true gentlemen are one in a thousand and the rest are not fit to lick a woman's shoes, and I say you judge too harshly. For although by nature men do, indeed, tend to be less than paragons of perfection, we have our redeeming traits, not the least of which is the special regard in which womanhood is generally held. This is especially true on military posts, where men outnumber women a hundred to one. I have often seen enlisted men gaze wistfully at an officer's wife, not with lust in their eyes but with the pure longing of lonely souls who dearly desire the most treasured of earthly blessings—the love of a good woman.

You can imagine, then, the solicitude with which Mrs. King was treated. I had only to express a need and it was met. I personally took it on myself to clean her wound, but I had Private Frederick apply the bandage. His father was a doctor, and he had helped treat the sick and wounded on occasion.

Six troopers had their hands full with the fire. Grass burns quickly. No sooner did they rushed out of the darkness and dumped the armloads they had collected onto the flames, than the grass was half-consumed and they had to rush back out again.

The whole while we ministered to Louisa and the two privates, I listened for shots or other sounds from off to the southwest, the direction Borke had fled. But there were none. Either Borke had given Zach King the slip, or King had yet to overtake them.

It would be foolish of me to give chase. They had too great a lead, and it was too dark to track. Common sense dictated I wait until dawn. And I must say, now that Louisa was safe, I did not feel the same urgency as before.

I squatted with my forearms across my knees and my chin on one of my wrists and was reflecting on the fickleness of life when a low groan heralded Lou's return to the living. I applied a cool damp cloth to her brow.

Her eyes opened. Reaching up, she blurted, "Where—? What—?"

"You've been shot, Mrs. King," I said formally. "Lie still. The wound has been dressed, but you have lost a lot of blood and are in no condition to move about."

"Lieutenant Pickforth?"

"None other. Consider me your humble servant." I bowed my head, but she had closed her eyes, and she groaned. "How do you feel?"

"Like I was stomped by a bull buffalo. My head hurts so, I can hardly think." She opened her eyes again and gripped my arm. "Zach! Where is he? And what about Borke's bunch?"

"My men and I drove them off." I must confess I felt giddy playing the hero. "As for your husband, he went after them, and would not turn back even when I yelled for him to do so."

"Zach rode off and left me?"

# David Thompson

There are times when having a conscience is more of a liability than an asset. "He thought you were dead. Blood was everywhere, and your pulse was so weak, anyone might have missed it."

"So he's all alone against the four of them?" Louisa tried to rise but couldn't do more than prop herself on her elbows. "You must go after him, Lieutanant. Or at the very least, send some of your men."

"It would be a waste of time, dear lady. We're not cats or owls. We can't see in the dark."

"But Zach might need help." She was growing frantic and tried to push herself higher. "If you won't go, lend me a horse and I'll go myself."

"You couldn't ride fifty yards in the shape you're in," I said, shaking my head. "No, for your own welfare, I insist you rest untill morning. Then we'll see if you've improved enough to handle a horse."

"But he's my *husband*." The way she said it, the way she accented the word, the way she infused it with the depth and breadth of the love in her heart, would do any man honor.

A smidgen of jealousy welled up in me. Silly, maybe, but nonetheless a fact. "All the more reason not to overexert yourself and make your condition worse. He would not want it, and I must act in his stead in his absence."

"You have no right," Louisa complained. Again she tried to stand, but after a minute she gave up and with a low whimper sank onto her back. "Confound the luck. If only that stray shot hadn't struck me."

"It wasn't Phineas Borke?"

"I don't think so, no. He had let go of me and was running toward their horses. I turned to Zach, and he was about to take me in his arms when my whole body went numb. That's the last I remember until now."

I saw her stare off into the night. Her torment was enough to melt a glacier. "Sergeant Fiske!" I hollered, and when he ran over, I barked, "Take ten men and ride southwest in search of Zach King."

"How far do we go, sir? And how do we find our way back again if we don't find him?"

"Can you guide your way by the constellations?" I asked. Our scout could, but then, it was second nature to frontiersmen.

"I can try, sir," Fiske said with a distinct lack of conviction.

The last thing I needed was some of my men lost on the prairie. "In that case, don't lose sight of our fire. When you have gone as far as you can without finding King, return straightaway." It was the best I could do under the circumstances.

"Thank you, Lieutenant," Louisa said.

I basked in the glow of her appreciation for all of two minutes. That was when she commented, "I can't stand the thought of something happening to him. Zach means the world to me." She paused. "Have you ever been in love, Lieutenant? So in love that you hurt inside when you are away from the one you care for?"

"I have never known affection that deep," I confessed.

"It's the greatest joy a person can experience. As if the two of you are one person whose hearts beat the same." Lou smiled, but not at me. "I never thought something like this would happen. If you had asked me ten years ago, I'd have said I would end my days a spinster. It's funny how life throws surprises at us, isn't it?"

I had just been thinking the very same thing. "Life is a perpetual fount of irony, that's for sure."

Louisa looked at me. "So you don't have a girl back home pining for you? A handsome gentleman like yourself?"

My ears were on fire. "All I have back home is a father who thinks God bestowed on him the right to boss others around as he sees fit, a mother who hides in her drawing room rather than confront problems, and a sister so in love with herself, she spends most of her time in front of a mirror."

"You sound bitter" was Louisa's observation.

"My father and I have never seen eye-to-eye. Ever since I can remember, he was always telling me what to do, always making my decisions for me instead of permitting me to learn for myself. Why, he would go so far as to decide which clothes I should wear and how I should have my hair cut. No aspect of my life was exempt from his scrutiny and his meddling." I am unsure why I told her all this. I never discussed my home life with anyone. I suppose it was due to my being somewhat smitten with her, which, let it be made clear, was a mystery in itself. She was hardly the type of woman I normally associate with. I was used to society's upper crust, to ladies who wear dresses, not buckskins. The women I dated were as fragrant as flowers. They did not smell of horse sweat. My social equals adorned themselves with exquisite diamonds and pearls, not quaint necklaces made of beads and shells. The ladies of my acquaintance liked to immerse themselves in the theater and art and other cultural pursuits, not in the rustic pastimes of the wilderness.

Louisa King was unlike any woman I had ever met. Does that explain my fascination with her? I have often heard it claimed that we are most attracted to those who are most different from us, and in that regard, it is hard to imagine anyone more different from me than she was.

"I am sorry to hear about your father," she was saying. "Did you ever sit down with him and make your feelings known?"

"Not in so many words, no." I did not see fit to relate the heated arguments my father and I had, culminating in the final explosion that resulted in my storming from our mansion and going to enlist.

"Maybe you should. I've found that the best way to settle spats is to talk them out. It works for Zach and me all the time."

"Have a lot of them, do you?" I fished for chinks in his armor.

"No, very few, actually." Lou smiled that dreamy smile of hers once more. "He and I get along together like two peas in a pod, which is strange given how different we are. It's even stranger when you consider my pa was killed by Indians—"

"He was?" I interrupted. "By Shoshones?"

"Goodness gracious, no. They wouldn't harm a white man if their lives depended on it." She started to shake her head, and grimaced. "I never did find out which tribe they belonged to. Even Zach didn't know, and he's familiar with pretty near all the tribes there are."

I was tired of hearing how wonderful her husband was. "Maybe you should try to get some rest."

"I'll sleep when your men come back. I'm too worried about Zach to do more than toss and turn."

Here she was, wounded and weak and in undeniable pain, and all she could think of was the man she loved. I envied Zach King at that moment as I have never envied anyone before or since. In a fit of pique I snapped at my men for letting the fire burn low, then

I rose and used the pretext of stretching my legs to go off into the dark a short distance.

What had come over me? You would think one of Cupid's tiny arrows had pierced me to the quick, the way I was acting. Which was absurd. Setting aside the different worlds we came from, there was the crucial fact that the woman was married. It was the same as having a ten-foot fence built around her with a sign posted that read, "Off Limits. Trespass at Your Own Risk." Trifling with married women was universally frowned on. It was one taboo that cut through all social and cultural layers.

I stood and faced into the brisk breeze and mentally scolded myself for being the biggest dunce this side of idiocy. Nothing could ever come of my schoolboyish yearnings. I had better deal with them and begin behaving as an officer was expected to behave.

I stayed away much longer than I should have. When I returned, Corporal Bittles was wearing a rut in the soil and some of the other men were nervously hefting their rifles. My presence calmed them. It made me realize the effect I had on their courage and their morale.

Coffee had been put on to boil, and I asked for a cup. It was weak. We were running low and had to ration what little was left.

Louisa had sat up and was propped against a saddle someone had kindly placed behind her for her benefit. She was sipping coffee and showed her white, even teeth in a warm smile. "I can't thank you enough for all you've done, Lieutenant."

"Don't make more of it than it is, Mrs. King."

"Oh, pshaw. You helped my husband rescue me, and for that I'll be eternally grateful."

She was under the mistaken impression that her husband and I had been working in concert, and I let her go on thinking that. We made small talk for an hour or so. I learned about her childhood in Virginia, and how her mother had loved living in the backwoods as much as her father. Which explained a lot. She was telling me about her tomboy years when hooves pounded the prairie and my patrol emerged from out of the night into the ring of firelight.

Sergeant Fiske slid down and saluted. "We never saw hide nor hair of them, sir. They had too much of a head start."

"Is that all?"

"We did hear some shots, but we couldn't tell which direction they came from." Fiske glanced at Louisa. "Right after that we heard a man scream. Then there was nothing. Nothing at all."

# Chapter Sixteen

By morning I had regained control of my emotions. I was angry at myself for my childish infatuation with Louisa King, and I chalked it up to the long and weary months my men and I had spent in the wilds. Months during which we had been deprived of female companionship.

How else to explain my silliness? Back east, I wouldn't look at Louisa King twice. Or so I flattered myself as we rode southwest the next day, the sun warm on our backs.

I could not help glancing at her, though. Repeatedly. She rode with an effortless grace rare in women, moving with the flow of her mount as if the two were one being. There was no denying that she was endowed with a degree of natural beauty. Her eyes, her lips, the sweep of her hair, they were sufficient to stir any man. Still, were I to stand her side by side with upper-crust members of the fairer gender, she would suffer by comparison.

All Louisa could think of was Zach. Several times she mentioned how worried she was, and how she couldn't wait until we overtook him and established that he was alive and well.

I couldn't wait, either, although I wrestled with myself over what I would do once we did.

I thought we might lose the trail, but it so happened that Louisa had picked up a few tracking skills from her in-laws, and pointed out prints to me now and again. We were nearing the foothills when she rose in her stirrups and pointed. "Look! There's a body!"

I swear that although I squinted with all my might, I saw no such thing. She slapped her legs against her horse, compelling me to do the same if we were to keep up with her. I was right behind her and could not help admiring how her legs and thighs molded to her saddle. Have I mentioned she was a superb rider?

Up ahead, dark winged shapes rose sluggishly into the air. Vultures, disturbed from their meal. Soon I saw what Louisa had seen. And yes, I admit that I secretly hoped it was Zach King. His death would solve everything. But when we drew rein, we were staring down at what was left of Thaddeus Sewell. He had been shot in the chest, right through the heart, and left for the scavengers. The vultures had eaten his eyes, nose, and lips, and had been tearing at his throat when we arrived.

"Sergeant Fiske, select a burial detail," I commanded. The longer we took overtaking King, the greater the chance Phineas Borke and his friends would solve my problem.

Predictably, Louisa said, "We don't have time for that! Leave him for the buzzards and coyotes."

"I'm sorry, Mrs. King. It's the Christian thing to do."

She was mad, but I refused to go on until the job was done. It consumed half an hour. Shortly thereafter we were threading through the foothills. By midday we were high up in the mountains, crossing a meadow bordered by a stream. I elected to halt.

"We can't afford to stop," Louisa complained. "We're hours behind them as it is."

"My dear Mrs. King," I said while dismounting, "we have our horses to think of. We have been pushing hard all morning, and they need to rest. Or would you rather we lose even more time when they collapse from exhaustion?" I was exaggerating, but I had a valid point and she knew it. She angrily swung down and walked toward the stream. I followed, but slowly and casually so as not to incite the slightest suspicion. "I hope you won't hold this against me."

She was on her knees, bending to dip her hands in the water. "You're only doing what you have to. Were it up to me, I'd ride my horse into the ground to save my husband." She splashed some water on her face, and the drops glistened like gems.

"I can't begin to imagine how rough this is on you," I pretended to sympathize. "It's beyond me how you have stayed in the wilderness so long."

Louisa twisted around, the sun bathing her in its rosy glow. She was positively breathtaking: her piercing, lovely eyes, her tanned complexion, the supple swell to her buckskins. I had to look away in order not to reveal my sentiments.

"I've always been at home in the woods, Lieutenant. As I told you, my pa was a backwoodsman, and ma was just as at home in the forest as he was. They passed their love of the wild places on to me, I reckon."

"Am I to gather you have never lived in a city or town? Not once your whole life?"

"Not once. And I never had a hankering to, either. Too many people, for one thing. When you're used to the quiet and peace of the deep woods, the hustle and bustle of a city is downright scary."

"You could become used to it if you tried," I suggested.

"Why would I want to when I have this?" She gestured at the regal peaks mantled with crowns of the purest snow. "I like the wide-open spaces. City life isn't for me, Lieutenant Pickforth."

"Call me Phil," I said, but she did not seem to hear.

"I don't like being hemmed in. I don't like living like a chicken in a coop, and that's exactly the feeling I get whenever I'm in a city or town for more than a few days. Ever been to St. Louis? There are so many people, you brush elbows when you walk down the street. There's no privacy, no place where a person can be alone with their own thoughts."

"That's not entirely true. Many cities have parks to stroll through. And there's always the privacy of one's own house or apartment."

"A few trees and a pond can't compare to mountains and lakes. And who would want to spend their days cooped up in a house or an apartment when they can roam as free as a buffalo?" Rising, she dabbed at her wet face with a sleeve. "No, city life isn't for me. I'd wither and die."

"But what if you were in love with someone who preferred the city over the country? Could you tolerate city life then?"

Her laugh was as lilting and melodious as musical chimes. "What a strange question! I already *am* in love with someone, remember? Zach is the only man I'll ever love, the only man I ever want or need."

The rush of blood to my head accounted for the mistake I now made. "Let's say, for the sake of argument, something were to happen to him? Could you ever love another?"

"What a terrible thing to suggest. I never want Zach to come to harm. I want the two of us to grow old together and one day be buried side by side by our children and grandchildren."

"Life does not always work out as we want."

"Why are you talking like this?" Her brow knit, and Louisa looked at me more intently than she ever had before.

I instantly turned and walked off. "I need to ensure our packhorses are being taken care of." I lied, since my men had the watering of the animals well in hand. I had been much too obvious. I hoped it had not aroused her suspicions, but several times over the next half an hour I caught her studying me when she thought I wouldn't notice.

When we mounted to ride on, she averted her face, and for the rest of the afternoon she made it a point to avoid meeting my gaze. That evening she sat across the fire from me but stared into the flames or off into the darkness or up at the stars. Anywhere except at me. Her tone when she spoke to me was far less friendly, and when I tried to draw her into conversation, she answered in monosyllables.

I fell into another funk. It was a failing of mine when things were not going as I wanted them to go. A habit carried over from childhood, I suppose, from the days when, as my father liked to say, I had been "spoiled rotten." Ironic that he should criticize me for being immature when he was the one who did most of the spoiling.

The next morning we were up and on the move by sunrise. To erase her unease, I determined to push hard and fast to convince her I was as anxious as she was to find her precious husband. The men grumbled, but enlisted men always grumble, although never loud enough for their officer to hear what they are saying.

Neither Borke nor King had stopped the previous night, which surprised me. "They'll kill their horses at the rate they're going," I commented at one point.

At last Louisa deigned to respond. "Borke knows he's a dead man if my husband catches him. He's making for a pass into Ute country. They're hoping Zach won't follow."

The Utes were hostiles, and one of the tribes I had been instructed to avoid at all costs. I mentioned this.

"You can turn around if you want once we reach the pass," Louisa said. "But I'm not. I won't rest again until I've set eyes on my husband." She stressed the last word for my benefit.

I pretended not to notice. The middle of the afternoon found us traversing a sawtooth ridge. I had twisted to verify that none of my men were straggling when distant popping sounds snapped my head around.

"Those were shots!" Louisa exclaimed, and she was off like a bolt of lightning, lashing her horse with her reins.

"Wait!" I called, in vain. I lashed my own reins to keep her in sight. She had plunged into dense, shadowy firs, and was swiftly climbing toward a distant cliff. I heard more shots, only louder. Zach King had Borke cornered.

Rounding a cluster of trees, I was disconcerted to discover that Louisa had disappeared. I straightened to try and spot her and nearly had my head removed from my shoulders by a low limb.

The loudest shot yet came from a slope to my left. I veered in that direction and glimpsed Louisa, hunched low over her saddle.

I glanced over my shoulder. My men were strung out over a quarter mile, some in clusters, others riding singly. The pack animals were even farther behind. We had lost all semblance of a military unit. By rights I was required to stop and have them reform, but my raging emotions smothered my logic and I raced headlong after Louisa King. I would gladly have followed her to the infernal gates of Hades if not for a man-made hornet that buzzed dangerously close to my head. A puff of smoke from the muzzle of a rifle told me where the shooter was—and illuminated my blunder in placing myself in their line of fire.

Reining into the underbrush, I swung down, jerked my rifle from its scabbard, and scrambled toward a group of boulders. Someone had beaten me there. I threw myself down beside Louisa as a slug whined past my ear. "Keep low!" I cautioned.

She had her head and neck exposed, and was frantically seeking Zach. "Where is he? He has to be here somewhere!"

Grabbing her arm, I hauled her down beside me. "Do that again and they'll put a bullet through your brain."

"Don't touch me!" she snarled, pulling loose.

Her vehemence stunned me. So did the spite I read in her eyes and the sneer curling her lips. "What has gotten into you?" I feigned innocence. "I'm only trying to keep you alive."

"Sure you are." She scooted several feet to the right and crouched behind a different boulder. "I meant what I just said. Lay a hand on me again and I'll scratch out your eyes."

"You're making no sense," I continued my sham. "I'm not your enemy. Borke is. He and his friends are the ones you need to watch out for."

"A woman always knows, Lieutenant."

"Knows what?"

Her stare made me uncomfortable, so I turned my attention to the rocks higher up. It occurred to me that there were more than three or four guns firing; it was more like nine or ten. Along about then I saw a buckskin-clad Indian pop up and snap off a quick shot. Not at us, but at another cluster of boulders forty yards farther. "What in the world?"

"Utes," Louisa said.

I could not have been more flabbergasted if she had informed me they were whales. "Where the devil did they come from?"

"Probably through the pass." She pointed at a niche in the cliff far above. "Ute hunting parties use it all the time on their way to the prairie after buffalo. Five will get you ten a hunting party spotted Borke and the two sides have been swapping shots. Our being here complicates things."

She had a flair for understatement. Some of the Utes were now shooting at my men, who sought cover and returned fire. The *crack-crack-crack* of rifles was almost constant.

"Where did they lay their hands on those guns?" I mused aloud.

"Maybe in trade for plews. Or maybe the Utes took them off of dead whites."

"Is there any chance they'll agree to a parley?" I had in mind tying my white handkerchief to my rifle.

"No. Years ago the Utes and some trappers tangled. A Ute chief agreed to meet with two of the whites under a flag of truce, and they killed him. Ever since, the Utes have distrusted all our kind."

Too often in this chaotic world, we must pay for the mistakes of others. I was debating what to do when Sergeant Fiske came scuttling up the slope like an ungainly crab.

"Sir! I've ordered the men to spread out in a skirmish line. Say the word and we'll wipe those hostiles out."

"Not without losing a few of our own," I responded. "Perhaps we can drive the Utes off without directly engaging them." I pointed at where the warriors were concentrated. "Spread word to our men that they are to concentrate their fire there on my signal."

"What about Borke and his friends?"

"First things first. The Utes are the greatest threat. Once we've dealt with them, we'll attend to Borke."

Although flat on his belly, Fiske saluted, then turned and scurried down into the firs. A couple of shots were thrown at him, but he made it unscathed.

"How many Utes do you think there are?" I inquired of Louisa.

"Half a dozen at most."

That tallied with my own deduction, and boded well for our attempt to drive them through the pass. Then she burst my bubble.

"Their village can't be far. I wouldn't put it past them to send a man for help, if they haven't already. In another hour or so this whole mountain could be swarming with more Utes than we can count."

# Chapter Seventeen

Our predicament was as bad as, if not worse than, our clash with the Piegans. There we were, hostiles to the right, cutthroats to the left, and there I was, my thinking addled by my unseemly passionate interest in Mrs. Louisa King to the point where I could not function as I should. I freely admit it was wrong of me to entertain the thoughts I did concerning her—thoughts more properly applied to saloon trollops.

In my defense, I submit that a man can no more choose those who will stir his heart than he can predict the future. Call it fate. Call it destiny. Call it magical, as the romanticists are wont to do. Whatever you call it, it exists, and once it has taken root in our innermost selves, keeping it in check is as impossible as stopping a raging avalanche.

In short, our inner cravings spur us into doing things we would never do otherwise. How else to explain my interest in Louisa King? Why else did I stay with her when my proper place was with my men? And most damning of all, why else was I entertaining the hope that Zach King had taken a bullet when I should be praying he made it through the fight alive?

My thoughts were derailed by an arrow that arced out of the blue and thudded between my legs. Another inch to either side and I'd have been scarred for life,

144

if not crippled. "We should take cover in the trees," I proposed.

"You go. I'm not budging until I find Zach."

Her devotion grated on my nerves. I had half a mind to seize her and drag her into the trees, but we would be riddled before we made it halfway. So I settled for saying, "You, madam, do not recognize when someone has your best interests at heart."

"And you, Pickforth, have buffalo shit for brains."

Those were her exact words. I swear it. Language fit for a sailor. Until that moment, despite her crude attire and her rough-hewn mannerisms, I had considered her a lady. Perhaps not in the same refined vein as those in my customary social circle, but a lady nonetheless. Suddenly I beheld her as she truly was and not as I imagined her to be. Suddenly I saw that she was no fit match for someone with my breeding and education. Suddenly I saw what I should have seen all along.

There are those who will say I was immature. That I was fickle. That my sheltered childhood had ill prepared me for the realities of the grown-up world. But I have learned it does not take much to turn like to dislike, or turn love to revulsion. Her eyes lost their appeal, her features lost their luster. She was the backwoods wife of a half-breed, nothing more, nothing less. And nowhere near as extraordinary as my misguided affections had made me believe.

Suddenly I was mad. Mad as hell, if you must know, and in need of something or someone to vent my anger on. Sergeant Fiske was awaiting my signal, which I now gladly gave, and at the slash of my arm, a thunderous volley was directed at the boulders concealing the Utes. More than twenty bullets spanged and whined and ricocheted, and were punctuated by a howl of pain. Again I raised my arm. Again I slashed it down. The second volley was as fearsome as the first, peppering the boulders like leaden hail.

The Utes did what any sensible person would do: They broke and ran. Within moments, five warriors were riding hell-bent for the pass while the sixth and a wounded companion, riding double, sought to catch up.

I raised my arm. Another volley would lay most of them low. But I didn't lower it. We had driven them off. That was enough. Slaying them would antagonize their tribe, and Colonel Templeton has been quite specific about not killing Indians when it could be avoided.

Waiting until the Utes were swallowed by pines, I gazed at the rocks harboring the cause of all we had been through. "Mr. Borke!" I bawled. "You have sixty seconds to show yourselves or suffer my wrath."

Borke was nothing if not consistent in his stupidity. "Go to hell, soldier boy! And take the rest of those jackasses with you!"

I have often wondered how some people manage to live as long as they do. Some have no more brains than an adobe brick; how they can get dressed without help mystifies me.

I suspected they would make a break for it even though they were well within rifle range of my men. The nearest cover was eighty feet west of the rocks, but that did not stop Clemens from breaking into the open. Bent low over his horse, he reined right and left to make himself harder to hit. Against a lone rifleman the ploy might work—not against twenty. The outcome was foreordained.

I gave the signal to fire. The volley smashed Clemens's animal to the earth. Catapulted from the saddle,

Clemens tumbled end over end. He made it to his feet but was leaking scarlet like a sieve and only staggered a few yards, his legs stiff and disjointed, before collapsing in a lifeless sprawl.

Cupping a hand to my mouth, I shouted, "Your turn, Borke. Or will it be Hyde who goes to meet his Maker?"

"Damn you to hell!" was the furious reply.

I grinned and glanced at Louisa King to let her know that as soon I had dealt with them, I would turn my attention to her husband. But she was gone! Forgetting that I was within range of Borke's and Hyde's rifles, I straightened and stepped past the boulders. It was inconceivable to me that she had slipped away without my noticing.

Another volley rang out. Not at my order, but at Sergeant Fiske's. I looked toward the high rocks and saw Phineas Borke duck for safety. He had been about to shoot me. "Reload!" I roared at my men. "Prepare to charge on my command!" We would overrun the miscreants.

"Hold on there, Lieutenant!" Jacob Hyde finally showed himself, his rifle held over his head. "I know when I'm licked."

"What about Mr. Borke?"

Hyde shifted toward a large boulder and said something. Whatever Borke answered brought a hoot of scorn and the remark "Get yourself killed! See if I care! I'm givin' up."

When Hyde had come close enough to hear without my shouting, I asked him, "Where is your horse?"

"Dead as dead can be, thanks to one of your boys in blue. Hit by a ricochet smack in the brainpan."

"If you don't mind," I said, relieving him of his rifle, pistols, and knife. Seconds later Sergeant Fiske and the majority of my men were at my side, and I handed the weapons over. "Will Borke surrender, or must we do this the hard way?"

"The lunkhead is afraid to show himself for fear the breed will blow out his wick," Hyde replied.

In the general excitement and press of events I had momentarily forgotten about Zach King. "Did anyone see where King's wife got to?" I inquired. No one had. "Bind Mr. Hyde," I directed.

"Is this really necessary, Lieutenant?" our former scout asked as a pair of husky troopers clamped his arms behind his back.

"Two of my men were wounded at Lizard Rock, and for all I know, you were responsible." I adopted my most imperious tone. "No one hurts those under me with impunity." Facing up the mountain, I shouted, "Mr. Borke, this is your last chance! I give you my word you will not come to harm if you desist in this foolishness and do not fire another shot."

His reply confirmed Hyde's statement. "What about Zach King? I'm not lookin' to cash in my chips if I can help it."

"I will have you escorted down. He won't dare shoot." To Sergeant Fiske I said, "Take six men. Surround him so King can't get a clear shot. The rest of you, cover them, and if you spot King, fire at will."

It was not long before Sergeant Fiske and his anxious charge started down. They brought Borke's horse along. What with the horse at his side and being ringed closely by my men, virtually no part of Borke was exposed. He made it down without mishap, and once he reached me, I had him hustled into the firs, his weapons confiscated, and his wrists secured with rope.

Borke voiced the same complaint as Hyde. "There's no need to truss me up, Lieutenant. I promise I won't cause you any trouble."

"I would be remiss in my duty if I took you at your word. You betrayed my trust when you kidnapped Mrs. King, and then compounded your villainy by shooting at us."

"Put yourself in my boots," Borke said. "I thought you were fixin' to let Zach King go free. I had to do what I did to lure King to me so I could avenge my brother."

"You're a simpleton, Mr. Borke. If all you wanted was revenge, you shouldn't have enlisted the army's aid. We go by the book, as we call it, and we do our duty proudly."

"There's that word again," Borke said in disgust.

"Which word?"

"Duty. It's how you always justify what you do."

Unwittingly, he had paid me the highest compliment a military man can be paid. Smiling, I said, "To a soldier, sir, duty comes before all else. Our personal feelings are of no consequence."

"What do you intend to do with us? Take us all the way back to Fort Leavenworth?"

I nodded. "Mr. Hyde and you will be turned over to the civil authorities and formally charged for your attempt on our lives. I will personally testify at your trial, and I hope they impose the severest sentence the law permits."

"You're a hard man, Pickforth."

Two compliments in as many minutes. I assembled my command, and we climbed on our horses and began our descent. I was eager to put as much distance as possible between us and the pass before the Utes returned, as I was sure they would after gathering re-inforcements.

"You did well back there," I praised Sergeant Fiske. "It will be so noted in my report to the colonel."

Fiske held his head a little higher and sat a little taller. "May I say, sir, that if you are ever sent out on another assignment or campaign, I would be honored to serve under you."

"Same here, sir," chimed in Corporal Bittles.

Four compliments. I was extremely pleased with myself. It is every officer's fondest dream to inspire confidence in his leadership and garner the implicit trust of those under him. But my euphoria was short-lived.

Phineas Borke raised his voice. "You know, don't you, Lieutenant, that Zach King won't let me leave this neck of the woods alive?"

I shifted in my saddle. "He has what he wanted. I imagine he and his wife will wait until we're gone, then head for their cabin."

Borke shook his head. "You don't know his kind like I do. They never let an enemy live if they can help it. I'm as good as dead." He tried to knee his horse up next to mine. "I beg you, Lieutenant, man to man, to untie me and give me a gun so I can defend myself."

"Nice try," I quipped. "But I learn fast, Mr. Borke, and I have learned there are no depths to which you will not stoop to get what you want. Which, in this case, is to escape."

"Think you know everything, don't you, boy?" This came from Jacob Hyde. "But Phineas is right. No crit-ter in all creation is as vengeful as a breed. Their blood is tainted from the day they're born."

"Do you honestly expect a graduate of Princeton to give credence to your superstitions?" I had to laugh.

"Breeds are vicious by nature. Ask anyone. Even Indians. They don't want nothin' to do with a half-blood, either."

"The Shoshones are on friendly terms with Zach King," I put the lie to his assertion.

"Only because he's Nate King's son and they hold his pa in high regard. The kid ain't like Nate, though. He's snake-mean when he's riled. And he hates whites."

"Perhaps that was true once," I said, "but his attitude has changed or he wouldn't be married to a white woman."

"I told you once before that you think you have all the answers," Hyde said scornfully. "Hell, you don't even know the questions."

After that we rode in silence. My men and our mounts were tired, but I intended to make camp for the night well out on the prairie. Now that I had made up my mind, I felt as if a great burden had been lifted from my shoulders. I was in extremely fine spirits and could not stop thinking about Fort Leavenworth, and what it would be like to once again enjoy a bath every day, and a glass or three of brandy every evening.

We were wending through the foothills when Phineas Borke started in on me again. "I'm curious, Lieutenant. What will your colonel say when he finds out you let Zach King slip through your fingers?"

"Neither I nor my men are trackers. And with Utes in the area, I deem it best to avoid a confrontation. Colonel Templeton will understand."

"The Utes aren't anywhere near King's valley. Why not go there and wait for him and his bitch to show up?"

"Give it a rest," I said.

"When will you get it through that thick Yankee skull of yours I can't rest so long as that damn breed is still alive?" Again Borke tried to urge his horse up next to mine, but Corporal Bittles was holding on to its reins and wouldn't let him. "Damn it, Pickforth! Listen to me! I'm beggin' you to do the duty you're always crowin' about and take Zach King back with us."

His carping had become tedious. I sighed and looked over my shoulder. "How long would you suggest we wait for them? A week? A month? Perhaps longer? We're short on supplies as it is. King and his wife are adept at living off the land. They can lie low until we're gone. Or they might go stay with his father or the Shoshones. The course of action you propose is pointless." I faced front. "Trust me, Mr. Borke. We have seen the last of Zachary King." And I couldn't be happier.

"Pardon me, sir," Sergeant Fiske interrupted. "But maybe we haven't."

"How's that again, Sergeant?"

Fiske was gazing back the way we came. He pointed at the last mountain we crossed. "We're being followed."

I looked, and although the horse was more than a mile away and I couldn't say if there was one rider or two, there was no mistaking the white markings: It was a paint.

# Chapter Eighteen

People are a mystery to me. Why they do the things they do defies rational thought. Take Zach King, for example. His wife was safe. Borke and Hyde were no longer a threat. I was leading my platoon homeward. What more could he ask for? Yet he was willing to risk his freedom, risk his marriage to a lovely woman, risk his very life, to satisfy his personal code of honor.

Several hours had gone by and we had not seen the paint again, but I knew King was still shadowing us. Borke had been right and I had been wrong, and I was man enough to admit it.

"Fat lot of good your apology does me," he said curtly. "I'm a gone goslin' unless you set me free."

"Rest easy, Mr. Borke. My men and I will protect you."

Beads of sweat were trickling down his moon face. "He'll kill me, I tell you, and there ain't a damn thing you can do to stop him."

We were well out on the prairie by then, and I commented, "I beg to differ. In open country like this, he can't get close enough except at night, and then I'll have you under guard."

"That won't stop a coon like Zach King. He's learned from the best. He'll slip in and out of your camp with you none the wiser, and leave me dead with my throat slit."

"Don't make him out to be more than he is," I said rather severely. "King is one man against many. You're perfectly safe with us."

Borke bowed his chin. "I'm as good as dead, is what I am, and you're a jackass if you don't see it."

"Amen, brother," Jacob Hyde said.

Sergeant Fiske jerked on the reins to the scout's sorrel. "That'll be enough out of the both of you! From here on out you'll speak when the lieutenant says you can, and not before."

"Or what, soldier?" Hyde taunted. "You'll rap our knuckles good and proper?"

"I'll have you gagged."

That shut them up.

The hours until twilight crawled by. We were crossing as flat a stretch as there ever was, the grass no taller than our knees, with no hills or washes or gullies anywhere to be had, when I declared, "We'll stop here for the night, gentlemen."

I doubled the number of sentries. I had our prisoners placed in my tent, with guards at each end and on both sides. I ordered the horses to be hobbled. And lastly, I instructed my men to bed down around the tent with their blankets practically touching.

As I stood complimenting myself on my precautions, it was obvious no one could get anywhere near Borke and Hyde without being detected.

Before turning in, I indulged in half a cup of weak coffee. By now we barely had any left. The same with most of our provisions. Added incentive for us to make a beeline for the post.

As I foresaw, the night was uneventful. So was the next, and the one after that. I thought it would prove to Borke that his fears were unfounded, but he became more worried instead of less.

"Don't you see? King is bidin' his time. Sooner or later you'll make a mistake, and that's when I'm done for."

Who can blame me for scoffing? I had things well in hand. Several more nights went by without mishap, but Borke would not stop fretting.

The next day, shortly before sunset, I called a halt beside a creek. I took the same steps as before to safeguard our prisoners. Then, as we were in need of fresh meat, I sent out six men, in pairs, to hunt game.

"Tonight will be the night," Borke commented as troopers were ushering them toward the tent.

"You are a born worrier," I said.

Jacob Hyde slowed. "This is what the breed has been waitin' for, Lieutenant." He nodded at the gurgling water. "Hear that? And the wind in the trees?" Cottonwoods framed both banks, and the breeze constantly rustled their leaves. "Your sentries won't hear him and your horses won't smell him."

Enough was enough. I expected this sort of nonsense from Borke, but not from the scout. Mockingly, I said, "And King will float on air over my men and enter the tent without my guards seeing him? I'm surprised at you, Mr. Hyde. And I'm willing to wager a dollar you'll still be alive come morning."

"Is that all my life is worth to you? Make it fifty dollars and you're on."

Four of the hunters I sent out returned empty-handed, but the last pair brought back a large doe lashed to a pole. The men were ravenous and gathered around to watch it be butchered. A few tried to help themselves to raw, bloody chunks, but I made them wait. Raw meat was known to make men sick.

Staring at them, though, I realized how gaunt they were. Not a man among them hadn't lost at least ten to fifteen pounds. They weren't skin and bones, but some were close to it. Most now had beards. The only reason I didn't was that I hated them; my father always had a beard, and I loathed how it itched my cheek when he hugged me. Dust caked our uniforms and many were in need of mending, but overall, given what we had gone through, I would say we were doing as well as circumstances allowed.

The meat took forever to roast. A quarter moon had risen and coyotes were yipping off across the plain when Sergeant Fiske sliced a thick, sizzling piece and brought it to me on my tin plate. You haven't heard a stomach growl unless you've heard mine. I'd swear it was as loud as a grizzly. Dispensing with my fork and knife, I picked it up, nearly burning my fingers, and sank my teeth into the hot, juicy flesh. I sat there without chewing, savoring the taste.

The men acted like starved cannibals. Some wolfed their food, others nibbled. Several moaned in ecstasy, they were so carried away.

Everyone was entitled to a portion, including the sentries and the tent guards. But I had them take turns so there was always someone keeping watch.

Only two troopers had yet to be fed when a commotion broke out behind the tent. "Lieutenant! Come quick!" Private Varnes hollered.

I was one of the first to reach him. His rifle was on the ground, and he was rubbing his chin and pointing at a slit in the canvas.

"I came back after getting my food, and he came flying out of there and slugged me!"

"Who?" I tried to delude myself into thinking it had to be Borke or Hyde.

"The half-breed, sir. He's faster than a rattler, that one."

Parting the slit, I ducked my head and entered. The meat in my stomach tried to climb back up my throat.

Phineas Borke lay on his back in a corner, his throat slit from ear to ear. The knife had sliced so deep, he was nearly decapitated. Blood poured from the stump, soaking his shirt. Lower down was another spreading stain, and bending, I saw its source. Bitter bile filled my mouth, and I almost gagged.

Whirling, I saw Jacob Hyde in the other corner. He was on his side, his body in a fetal position. I had to force myself to grip his shoulder and roll him over. His neck was slick with blood, but to my amazement, he opened his eyes and sat up.

"About damn time! I thought I was done for!"

"But he slit your throat!" I blurted.

"He tried. But he heard the guard and had to work fast, and all he did was crease me. I pretended to be dead so he wouldn't try again."

Sergeant Fiske and several troopers had followed me in. "Bring Mr. Hyde to the fire so we can bandage him," I commanded them, and once in the light, I confirmed that the wound was superficial. "You were lucky."

Hyde was also furious. "No thanks to you, you damned know-it-all! Phineas is dead because you were too stubborn to listen to us. Now King will bide his time until he can finish me off, same as he did Borke."

"I've made one mistake. I won't make another."

"What's that supposed to mean?" Hyde snapped.

"It means that at first light we are going after Zachary King."

"As if you have a prayer of catching him."

"King has made two mistake of his own," I noted. "He left you alive to track for us. And he and his wife are riding double."

Or so I thought until the next morning when it was discovered that one of our horses was missing. It was another mistake on King's part. Two horses leave more sign than one.

Jacob Hyde said that he could follow the trail blindfolded, and I tended to believe him. The man was a cad, but he was a competent frontiersman. By nine A.M. we had found the charred embers of the small fire the Kings had made the previous night.

"They lit out before dawn, Lieutenant," Hyde revealed. "Travelin' east."

"They would be better off making for the mountains," I observed.

Hyde touched the bandage on his throat. "The breed must know I'm still alive and he aims to finish what he started. They're headin' east to get ahead of us and look for a likely spot to do the job."

"Then that's their fourth lapse in judgment. Lead on, Mr. Hyde. And don't spare the reins."

By noon we had narrowed the gap to less than an hour.

"They're takin' their sweet time," Jacob Hyde remarked. "They don't know we're after them yet, but they will soon."

Sure enough, it wasn't long before their horses changed from a walk to a trot.

"See here? They stopped to rest and spotted us." Hyde was on his knees, examining some tracks. "They're no more than ten minutes ahead of us."

That wasn't much, but we had to be a lot closer before I dared give our mounts their heads. Our horses were as tired as we were. It didn't lessen my confidence, though. "We have them now!" I crowed.

Jacob Hyde swung onto his sorrel. "Anyone else but Zach King, and I'd agree. But he's as much Indian as he is white, and knows tricks even I don't know."

That became apparent when the tracks we were following disappeared. One moment they were so plain even I could follow them, and the next they seemed to end in thin air. "How is this possible?" I demanded.

"It's not." Hyde sprang down and dropped onto all fours. "See these bent blades of grass? King cut up a blanket and wrapped the pieces around his pinto's hooves. But he can't shake us this way."

Still, the ploy slowed us down. Time and time again Jacob Hyde had to dismount to confirm that we hadn't lost the trail. By my pocket watch it was past two in the afternoon and we were plodding along under the hot sun when Hyde suddenly reined up and thrust out an arm.

"There, Lieutenant! That's them!"

King and Louisa hadn't spotted us yet. Sergeant Fiske was all for charging them, but I refused permission. "Patience, Sergeant. Let's try to get a little closer."

The horse they had stolen was limping. I mentioned this to Hyde, and he nodded. "When a man's luck turns bad, it turns bad all the way. Out of all the horses the breed had to choose from, he picked one that's comin' up lame."

My father would disagree. He was fond of saying that each of us makes our own luck. But it certainly did seem as if the Kings were jinxed.

"Wish I had me a Kentucky long rifle," Jacob Hyde said. "I could drop them from their saddles."

Like most frontiersmen, Hyde had manure dribbling from his ears. At that juncture the range to our quarry was half a mile. No marksman alive could make such a shot.

Suddenly Corporal Bittles exclaimed, "Look, sir! They've seen us!"

King and his wife had turned their horses broadside to us. But only for a few fleeting seconds. Wheeling, they spurred to a gallop and sped eastward.

I ordered six men to stay with the pack animals. The rest accompanied me at a trot. We lost some ground but never lost sight of the Kings. Soon they reined up, and Louisa switched from the horse that was going lame to the paint.

"They can't outrun us riding double, sir," Sergeant Fiske stated.

The paint had stamina, I'll say that for it. Burdened as it was, it outpaced us for three or four miles. Then fatigue took its tool and the paint slowed.

I could imagine Zachary King's frustration. I wondered if he would make a fight of it, or if his wife's cooler head would prevail and he would throw down his weapons and give himself up. It mattered little to me, either way, at this point. I had come to terms with myself.

They were only a few hundred yards ahead when King's paint whinnied and its hindquarters abruptly rose into the air. King and Louisa were flung head over heels. I thought the paint came down on top of them, but when we got there I saw they had been spared being crushed to death.

A prairie dog town was to blame. The paint had stepped into a burrow, and momentum and gravity did the rest. Its front leg was shattered, shards of white bone sticking out like jagged spears, and it thrashed and nickered in agony.

Zach King lay dazed, a knot on his forehead the size of a goose egg. Although rattled by her fall, Louisa had recovered, and as we rode up, she scrambled toward her husband's rifle. Sergeant Fiske beat her to it. Thwarted, she lunged for the pistols at her husband's waist, then screeched like a wildcat when two of my men seized her. "Let go!" she shrieked, kicking at their shins and knees.

By then I had climbed down. With my hands clasped behind my back, I walked over, as calmly as could be, and slapped her across the face. "That will be quite enough, Mrs. King. I grant you are not a lady. But it is in your best interests to behave like one."

Shock turned Louisa to stone.

The very next instant, Zach King groaned, stirred, and sat up. He was ringed by rifles, but he showed no alarm. In fact, he grinned at me and said, "I reckon my string has about played out."

"That it has," I agreed.

Louisa clutched at the only straw she had. "Please, Lieutenant! You can't blame him! Not after what Borke and the others did."

I refused to look at her. "There are limits, Mrs. King. A line that, once crossed, cannot be excused."

"Don't!" she pleaded. "I'm begging you."

I nodded, and my men hauled her husband to his feet. He stood tall, I'll say that for him, defiance blazing in his eyes. "Zachary King," I began. "By the authority of the United States government, pursuant to the powers invested in me as an officer in the United State Army, I hereby take you into custody for the massacre committed at the Green River trading post and for the heinous murder of Phineas Borke. You will be taken to Fort Leavenworth, and once there, bound over for trial." I paused, and smiled. "I hope to God they hang you."

# Afterword

*Seven weeks later, Pickforth's bedraggled platoon arrived at Fort Leavenworth. As for the trial and its aftermath, that is the subject of our next tale.*

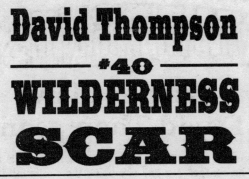

# David Thompson
## #40
# WILDERNESS
# SCAR

The vast American frontier is filled with unimaginable beauty, natural wonders . . . and incredible danger. When a huge grizzly bear begins to threaten the native Utes, they turn to their friend Nate King for help. Who better to trap a grizzly than the legendary "Grizzly Killer," as Nate is known among the Shoshones? Nate's reputation as a hunter and tracker has spread throughout his mountain home. But as the famous frontiersman sets out to end the reign of terror caused by the rogue bear, he quickly sees that he will need all of his renowned skills and abilities. This is no ordinary grizzly, and it will take a far-from-ordinary man to kill it.

# WILDERNESS

## Fang & Claw
## David Thompson

To survive in the untamed wilderness a man needs all the friends he can get. No one can battle the continual dangers on his own. Even a fearless frontiersman like Nate King needs help now and then and he's always ready to give it when it's needed. So when an elderly Shoshone warrior comes to Nate asking for help, Nate agrees to lend a hand. The old warrior knows he doesn't have long to live and he wants to die in the remote canyon where his true love was killed many years before, slain by a giant bear straight out of Shoshone myth. No Shoshone will dare accompany the old warrior, so he and Nate will brave the dreaded canyon alone. And as Nate soon learns the hard way, some legends are far better left undisturbed.

___4862-0                          $3.99 US/$4.99 CAN

**Dorchester Publishing Co., Inc.**
**P.O. Box 6640**
**Wayne, PA 19087-8640**

Please add $2.50 for shipping and handling for the first book and $.75 for each book thereafter. NY, NYC, and PA residents, please add appropriate sales tax. No cash, stamps, or C.O.D.s. All orders shipped within 6 weeks via postal service book rate. Canadian orders require $2.50 extra postage and must be paid in U.S. dollars through a U.S. banking facility.

Name_____
Address_____
City_____State_____ Zip_____
I have enclosed $ _____ in payment for the checked book(s).
Payment <u>must</u> accompany all orders. ☐ Please send a free catalog.
        CHECK OUT OUR WEBSITE! www.dorchesterpub.com

# PETER DAWSON

# LONE RIDER FROM TEXAS

The heart of the American West lives in Peter Dawson's stories, with characters who blaze a trail over a land of frontier dreams and across a country coming of age. Whether it tells of the attempt of an outlaw father to save the life of his son, who has become an officer of the law, or a shotgun guard who is forced to choose between a seemingly impossible love and involvement in a stagecoach robbery, each of these seven stories embodies the dramatic struggles that made the American frontier so unique and its people the stuff of legend.

------------------------------------